BURNING THE NIGHT

PRAISE FOR
BURNING THE NIGHT

"*Burning the Night* begins with fire; the blackened sketches and journal pages of an artist fluttering down to become memories. Like these charred artefacts, Huser's eloquent words become a puzzle on the pages, with pieces of the narrative fitting together to slowly reveal the lives of Aunt Harriet and of Curtis. This is the work of a master storyteller."

—BETTY JANE HEGERAT, AUTHOR OF *THE BOY*

"This is a story of inner and outer sight, of blindness both acquired and enforced on us by society. Huser is a sensitive yet ruthless observer of human nature."

—ALISON WATT, AUTHOR OF *DAZZLE PATTERNS*

"Like a vivid shock of red in a sepia photo or the lurid love letter of an historical icon, *Burning the Night* unshackles the past from our dusty preconceptions, bringing it roaring into the full-colour present with the force of an atom bomb. Painting on a wide canvas of famous Canadian history, Huser perfectly conjures that feeling we get when we see images of our old relatives as young adults and think, 'Wow, they were just like us.'"

—BRUCE CINNAMON, AUTHOR OF *THE MELTING QUEEN*

BURNING THE NIGHT

a novel

GLEN HUSER

NEWEST PRESS
EDMONTON, AB

Library and Archives Canada Cataloguing in Publication

Title: Burning the night / Glen Huser.
Names: Huser, Glen, author.
Identifiers: Canadiana (print) 20200267493 | Canadiana (ebook) 20200267507 | ISBN 9781774390115 (softcover) | ISBN 9781774390122 (EPUB) | ISBN 9781774390139 (Kindle)
Classification: LCC PS8565.U823 B87 2021 | DDC C813/.54—dc23

NeWest Press wishes to acknowledge that the land on which we operate is Treaty 6 territory and a traditional meeting ground and home for many Indigenous Peoples, including Cree, Saulteaux, Niitsitapi (Blackfoot), Métis, and Nakota Sioux.

Board Editor: Sheila Pratt
Cover design & typesetting: Kate Hargreaves
Author photograph: Perspectives Photography Studio

Canada Council for the Arts   Conseil des Arts du Canada   Funded by the Government of Canada   Financé par le gouvernement du Canada   Canadä

access©   Alberta Government   Edmonton   edmonton arts council

NeWest Press acknowledges the Canada Council for the Arts, the Alberta Foundation for the Arts, and the Edmonton Arts Council for support of our publishing program. This project is funded in part by the Government of Canada.

NeWest Press

201, 8540 – 109 Street
Edmonton, AB T6G 1E6
780.432.9427
www.newestpress.com

No bison were harmed in the making of this book.
PRINTED AND BOUND IN CANADA
1 2 3 4 5 23 22 21

In memory of Ellis and the years we had together

Who stares too long
At stars may err
In thinking she
Is like a star
Burning the night
In slow delight

—Theodore Roethke
Love Has Me Haunted

SOME OF THE PAPERS, I IMAGINED—THOSE THAT HAD NOT been immediately driven to ground by the black, oily rain—fell, in that odd, unhurried way that airborne papers have, drifting past the blazing islands of debris, fluttering to rest in the grass where moisture fixed and darkened the charcoal lines, the sinuous trunk of a jack pine, the slope of a Toronto roof, the curve of a man's hip. Hours later, when the fires burned in on themselves and the snow came with a white, ashy fury, water hardened into barnacled ice, anchoring the papers so that, when fingers pulled at them, they were released with odd, torn patterns.

Others flew, like strange birds—cream manila, cartridge white, rag grey—into the racing currents of air, the giant exhalation, the gasp. These settled, finally, into nests of cracked porcelain, tumbled brick, kindled wood. Or they became lost in debris-strewn alleys, the yards, the shattered rime of the marsh grass along the beach.

In my mind's eye, I could see the leather case falling with curtains and shards of glass, the tiny bottles and dresser-top jars, a tin coffee pot, that small oil painting on a piece of board. How long did it take for fire to travel through the trail of splintered wood that had been Mrs. McTavish's house? Find the shattered washstand where the case had come to rest? The small portfolio was durable, though, and flames only managed to work their way into one corner before its bonfire underpinnings collapsed and it tumbled into the yard. The drawings tucked within barely damaged, seeming only to have been gnawed at in one corner by a rodent with fire in its teeth.

"I kept it all close by me," Aunt Harriet told me. "The case with its journal, sketches and photographs tucked inside, resting on top of a ragged collection of the drawings people found. You should have heard the nurses complaining that it got charcoal and chalk all over the bedding and my clothing.

"Hospital volunteers, or Mrs. McTavish, when she visited, would do their best to describe their sequence. I thought I could remember the order in which the papers lay. On top were the ones from inside the case only burned in one corner, and then there were a few Mrs. McTavish retrieved from her front yard. The rest? Found by people sifting through debris. Added over several days.

"Of course it was only a matter of time until I accidentally knocked everything over. When the papers were gathered up, I had no way of knowing which was which. The loose ones that people found here and there were in with those that had been in the case. One of the hospital aides offered to iron the most crumpled pieces of artwork for me but I said no, I wanted to be able to feel the ridges, the rips and torn edges.

"The odd thing was that, in time, I got to know the shapes of the damage as well as I could remember the drawings and paintings themselves. That one, with a kind of spoon-shape torn out—it's the figure of a soldier, isn't it? I suppose there's not much left of the actual charcoal sketch, but I imagine you can see his hands. Yes, I've been told, I think, his hands, and part of his uniform. That one was found half a mile away. Would never have been picked up, I suppose, if it hadn't been for that little article in the newspaper. Church ladies or Mrs. McTavish would come in and read the papers to me, and, of course, there were stories to fill the pages for months on end. This one, with a crescent moon shape near the top—you might wonder what that is, but I think it's a sketch of driftwood washed up on Kitsilano Beach."

Along the jagged opening, the twisted branches reach out, dead wood on sand, sand marked with small stains of—what? Blood? Oil? The liver spots of age?

CHAPTER 1

WHAT WAS HER AGE WHEN I FIRST SAW HER? Fifty-five? She was not that much older than my mother—a few years—but, to my eleven-year-old eyes she was an old woman. I was one of those children, though, who are at ease with adults, and from that first visit, I believe, we bonded in a strange, ineffable way—a spell was cast that caught me and held me for all the time I knew her and well past her death. Walter would say there are vestiges of it still. The way I frame a sentence. My affection for old bits of furniture, pictures, books from the time of the First World War. A violin piece that might well have been played in a Vancouver parlour as men waded through trench mud in the Somme.

"Ashes from the past," he says, the words edged with affectionate indulgence.

Like Aunt Harriet, I had spent a good deal of my life in blindness, but a blindness of my own selection.

In hindsight, I can see we were kindred spirits, the old woman and the young man, with our dreams and denials.

I remember visiting her only once before her husband, my uncle Hartley, died and I left my own family to move to the city. My mother disapproved of Harriet Coleman. In her mind was the certainty that Harriet had somehow used her handicap to trap her brother Hartley into a fruitless marriage. It was a thought that continued to rankle over the years: that Hartley should have raised an illegitimate child and provided for a woman who spent most of her waking hours reading, tracing Braille characters with one hand while she chain-smoked with the other. Hartley Coleman, in my mother's opinion, could have had his pick of women.

Of the visit in question, perhaps because my mother would speak of it in the same voice with which she spoke of Communist aggression in Korea and Catholic bingos in St. Paul, I recall a good deal. With my brother and myself in tow, my face still numb from the ministrations of a dentist in the Tegler Block, we made the trip from downtown Edmonton to the South Side.

It was a day heavy with heat, slaked with the sound unusual to us of the continuous movement of traffic. After we got off the trolley, we straggled along a side street south of Whyte Avenue and stopped at a small stucco bungalow. My brother and I fought over who should be allowed to ring the doorbell, an altercation that led to its being activated two or three times by flailing fists and jabbing elbows before we were cuffed away from it. At this point, my mother looked like she had spent the morning herself underneath the dentist's drill. She swept back a strand of hair that had escaped from her church-and-town hat and fixed us with a look that indicated our weekly allowances were in peril.

"Shitheel," my brother hissed in my ear.

"Dinkbrain." I shot back, practicing the lip control of ventriloquism.

A woman with a tea towel in one hand opened the door. She looked at us quizzically.

"Is Mr. Coleman in?" My mother stationed herself in front of the two of us.

"He's not home." The woman protectively blocked the door. "Can I do something for you?"

"Mrs. Coleman. Is she home?" We recognized a rasp-edge to our mother's question. At home we would have taken it as a cue to disappear.

"Who is it, Jean?" The voice, issuing against the soft heat of the early afternoon startled me with its clarity. Coming from the recesses of the house, it had the kind of definition and presence I associated with film actresses whose words drifted into the cocooned darkness of the Legion Hall in Yarrow on Saturday nights.

"It's Violet," my mother shouted, "and Bradley and Curtis."

"Oh my." The clear, distant voice. "Come on in. Jean, have them come in." We followed her to a kind of sitting room, with its Venetian blinds drawn against the invasive sunlight of a southwestern exposure. It took a minute for my eyes to become accustomed to the filtered light, and then I saw Uncle Hart's wife sitting in an easy chair in the

far corner. She looked like some kind of exotic, alien creature to me, a creature with dark glasses, two bottle-green
eyes. Sure enough she held a book open in her lap.

"Violet." She marked her place in the book with a
piece of ribbon, closed it, and set it on a small round table
at her side. "Jean, this is Hart's sister and her boys. What
a surprise. Hart didn't mention anything."

"We didn't know ourselves—that we were coming in.
But Curtis had a bad toothache and Mr. Jenkins who runs
the grocery store in Yarrow was making the trip anyway so
we had a ride and the dentist, when I phoned, was able to fit
us in. He won't be going back today but we'll catch the bus.
Hart mentioned he was taking some time off this month
and I thought maybe this might be one of the holidays, you
know, and we'd get to see him, and you of course. The boys
have only been to the city once before and we've none of
us seen where Hart lives ..." Our mother was never one to
run on. I think both Bradley and I listened to this spill of
explanation with something close to amazement.

Aunt Harriet rose from her chair. And while she
couldn't see our mother, she divined where she was
standing, barely in from the door. Tall and long-legged, it
took the blind woman only a couple of steps to reach her
and wrap her arms around her in a hug.

Mom uttered a little gasp. Her own hands, one clutching her purse and a shopping bag—we'd spent some time
in Kresge's next door to the dentist's after my tooth had
been filled—remained at her side.

"Hart did take holidays but he's out of town. For a
couple of days. Fishing with his sales manager. I'm so

sorry." Aunt Harriet released Mom from the hug. "Please, find a place to sit."

The woman who had let us in—Jean—moved some mending from the sofa and nodded toward a couple of upholstered chairs.

The next few minutes of conversation were lost in my sudden and pressing concern to find a washroom. Bradley smiled angelically, but with evil knowledge, as he watched me squirm and cross and uncross my legs. We were invited up to Aunt Harriet's chair so that she could trace our facial features with her fingertips. "Bradley has his uncle's jaw," she decided. By the time she was ready to feel my face, I was so in need of a facility that no part of my body would remain motionless for even a second.

"For heaven's sake, stand still," my mother said.

"He's got to pee," said Bradley.

I was grateful that Aunt Harriet could not see the shade of crimson I was turning. She laughed, a tinkling, beautiful laugh that was nearly disastrous to my bladder. Jean was called and I was shown to the bathroom tucked between the dining room and a bedroom. I inhaled the smell of scented soap and tobacco as I relieved myself into the shining porcelain and water of the city commode. Running water had not yet made its way to the street we lived on in Yarrow, Alberta.

When I returned, I heard my mother saying, "After all this time, we keep expecting you'll come with Hart when he visits."

"I'm not a good traveller." Aunt Harriet smiled. It seemed she was about to say something more, but instead she put the cigarette to her mouth again and for a minute there was nothing but silence and smoke.

"And Phip? What is he up to these days?"

"Phip? He's at work too. And he's got his own apartment now."

In the two years since his parents had moved to Edmonton, we'd come to know Phip, Uncle Hartley's stepson. The last time he'd been to Yarrow, he'd taken in a dance at the Legion Hall.

"Dancing's the most fun you can have that you can talk about in a mixed crowd," Phip had laughed. He seemed to have music running in his veins as he jigged around our living room to radio tunes, warming up to the prospect of the evening. Bradley and I begged to go too, but my mother had stuck to her guns. In her parental calculation, you needed to be fourteen to go to a public dance, and Bradley and I both had a ways to go.

"When you see him, tell him not to be a stranger," my mother said and I felt the heft of that last phrase, the way my mother put it out there—something Harriet could not fail to recognize as a criticism.

There was another weighted silence.

Although Harriet Coleman had no way of seeing where she was looking, I sensed my mother trying to keep from staring at her sister-in-law. Mom's gaze settled on Bradley, who had his arms crossed over his chest, and whose gaze in turn was focused on the table where a coffee cup and the remains of a sandwich sat beside the library book and cigarette box. Bradley was pop-eyed with excitement. He kicked me as I sat down again and nodded toward the tabletop. A large black beetle made its way leisurely across the sandwich plate, stopping to inspect a shred of lettuce. I wondered what Aunt Harriet would make of my mother's sudden intake of breath followed by a noise that sounded to me like a whimper.

Jean came in at that moment. "Aah," she said, "a wee beastie." She scooted the bug into a saucer and carried it out.

"What?" Aunt Harriet continued smoking, hardly moving.

"A bug," said Bradley.

Aunt Harriet laughed. "Hart thinks they have a secret passageway into the house. He gets mad at Jean because she keeps putting them back outside."

My mother, I could see, supported her brother's stance.

"Tell me about yourself, Bradley." Aunt Harriet had finished her cigarette and, removing her glasses, massaged the bridge of her nose. The removal of the glasses made the network of scars that covered her face more noticeable.

"Uh," Bradley gurgled and looked desperately at our mother.

"Bradley loves sports." Our mother still eyed the table anxiously as if a trail of the beetle's relatives waited close by. "He's a lot like Hartley in that way. Hartley was the best baseball pitcher around when he was younger."

I had trouble imagining this. The few times I had seen Uncle Hartley he seemed to have trouble moving his huge frame at a walk, never mind a run.

"And Curtis?"

"Oh, Curtis is our scribbler. Always writing something or doodling pictures." My mother laughed apologetically.

We generally depend on a person's eyes to indicate interest, but somehow Aunt Harriet managed to do it with her body. Her head craned forward; her hands grasped the arms of the easy chair.

"You write and draw," she said.

I nodded and Bradley kicked me in the shins again. "She can't see you jerking your dumb neck."

"A little," I muttered. There was a tingling feeling in my lips as the freezing began to wear away.

"Can you see the pictures over on this wall?" She gestured to an alcove just to the left of her chair. There were four framed pictures—three sketches in chalk ranked around a small oil painting of dark blackish-purple trees foregrounded against a blaze of distant autumn brush. One of the chalk sketches was of an old man in an elaborate, carved chair, looking up from a book he was reading. Another was a still life with a Chinese vase filled with chrysanthemums, a couple of golden pears and a green apple beside the bouquet.

But it was the third picture that caught both Bradley's and my attention. It was the largest of the four, chalky pencil on cream-coloured paper revealing a naked lady reclining on a sofa. I heard Bradley give a snort of amazement. The woman was wondrously displayed to us, her head tilted as if she was looking into the eyes of someone she knew intimately, her hair falling in waves over breasts that were full. The artist's pencil seemed to have lingered over the nipples, the delta of pubic hair. I stood awestruck, my mouth open.

"Jesus Christ," Bradley said, just loud enough for me to hear.

Our mother too, by this time, had made her way over to view the pictures. She made a small noise that made me think of someone experiencing a stomach cramp.

Looking at the sketch now, I realize my eleven-year-old eyes were riveted to the body's sexual revelation. The pencil turning against a knee is much darker and more forceful than its tracing of a nipple. But back at Aunt Harriet's in 1953, Bradley and I were not looking at the naked lady's knees. Nor was, I imagine, my mother.

"The sketches were done by Phillip Pariston." A softness came into Aunt Harriet's voice. "The old gentleman was his grandfather. Phillip—Phip's dad—loved him dearly and it's a portrait I remember well. It was always the first thing you would see among the loose papers in his small portfolio, which had been a gift from old Mr. Pariston. I think Phip trimmed the bit of damage from the bottom of the page before he got it framed."

Aunt Harriet paused. Was she going to tell us about the other sketches too? The flowers and fruit? The naked lady?

"That oil painting was given to him by Tom Thomson. I have been offered a fair amount of money for that one, but I like to keep it. It's a painting I can remember with my fingers."

At that point, Jean came in bearing a tray with tea for the women and glasses of cherry soda for Bradley and me. The talk turned to questions of sugar and cream and where to place cups and who would like an ice cream wafer. Discussion of the alcove pictures ceased and was not picked up again.

"I WOULDN'T GIVE TWO CENTS FOR ANY OF THEM," MY mother told Bradley and me over a late lunch at the bus terminal café. "That one is just globs of paint. And that other one—" She was, for a minute, at a loss for words. "Well—it's disgusting. I can't believe Hartley agreed to let something like that up on a living-room wall. But then he never says anything, does he?"

Once Bradley and I had finished our glasses of pop, my mother had uttered one of the few lies of her life and declared, as Aunt Harriet pressed us to stay, that our bus back to Yarrow was leaving in exactly one hour. The departure time was closer to three hours. Our walk from the streetcar to the depot had been fast-paced and hot. Bradley and I kept our distance. In the depot, we pretended we couldn't see the tears of frustration in Mom's eyes that finally welled up as she bit into her egg-salad sandwich.

"It's a blessing," she muttered, "your grandmother never got to see what Hart has had to live with."

On the way home, Bradley and I had a Greyhound seat to ourselves, several rows back from our mother who, because she got carsick easily, had taken the seat right behind the bus driver.

"Do you think someone really sat on a couch all naked," Bradley whispered, "and got her picture drawn?"

"Of course," I answered. Even though Bradley was a year older than me, he actually believed that, because I always had my nose in a book, I knew more than he did about some things. "Artists do it all the time. They're like doctors; they study the human body."

"Was Phip's dad an artist?"

"Sure. Weren't you listening at all?" I was having trouble keeping my eyes open. Bradley, too, was giving in to a succession of yawns. With our early rising to get to the city it had already been a long day.

I woke up when the bus pulled in and stopped at one of the small villages that dotted the route from Edmonton to Yarrow. Bradley continued snoring softly. When I noticed our mother half-risen from her front seat to get a look back at us, I wiggled some fingers at her that I hoped indicated we were alive and well. The bus idled with sub-dued power as the driver disgorged bags from an under-belly below my window. A man smelling of garlic got on and sat behind me and then the door wheezed shut and we were back on the highway. It was early evening and a haze of smoke smudged the passing farms and fields and intermittent clusters of ragged swamp pines.

In the few minutes that it took to fall back asleep, I called the sketch of the nude to my mind. It was crazy for a blind woman to have a picture of a naked lady on her wall. Or was it? On our own walls there were framed pictures out of the Toronto Star Weekly, dramatic outdoor scenes that my father liked of hunters coming suddenly on a grizzly around a mountain bend, or elk nuzzling a sunset. My mother had balanced these with painted plaster-of-Paris plaques of geese in flight and some gilt-rimmed Biblical prints: Christ in Gethsemane; Jesus as a shepherd. But I had discovered pages of unclad figures in encyclopedias and art history books in the Yarrow Public Library. Where did these naked figures exist apart from the reference pages? Had they ever hung on someone's wall?

Just as sleep was smoothing away these questions and I was yielding to the drone of the bus hurtling along the gravel road, I suddenly realized something. Bits of the afternoon melded together and hardened like the amalgam in my upper back tooth. With certainty I knew that the naked lady was Aunt Harriet herself, Aunt Harriet from decades before my own birth. It was something my mother must have realized too, adding to her sense of outrage.

As I stood by Aunt Harriet's chair when we were saying our goodbyes, she clasped my hand and whispered, "You have the gift." The words and the hand touched me again, spilling through the erratic engine noise of the Greyhound. "You have the gift. Nourish it. Don't ever let it be taken from you."

CHAPTER 2

I N THE DAYS FOLLOWING THAT VISIT TO EDMONTON, I plagued my mother with questions about Uncle Hartley's blind wife. Mom was not a loquacious woman, though, and it seemed, when it came to Uncle Hartley's marriage, there were more spaces than usual in her answers to my barrage of questioning. How she became blind, of course, I knew.

"But how did they meet? Uncle Hart and her—I mean, a blind person. Did he bump into her?" I'd stationed myself on a kitchen stool, keeping my mother company while she ironed.

"Don't be silly. If he told me, I can't remember. Besides, it's no affair of ours."

"But—"

"I think she'd been sick."

"Sick? Her eyes?"

My mother briefly twirled her fingers against her temple. "In her mind too, I think."

"But she's not now. Is she?"

Mom shrugged her shoulders and returned to her ironing. "It's none of our business."

But it was our business, I reflected. Family was always the business of other family, wasn't it? Sick in the mind. The extraordinariness of it tantalized my thoughts. If my mother was a sparse source of information, I would find an opportunity to quiz my father.

He ran a second-hand shop on the corner of a block of businesses along Yarrow's Main Street. One corner of the store was dedicated to the shop work he liked to do, repairing old bits of furniture, creating nut bowls and lamp stands. A turning lathe and table saw created dust and shavings and it was one of my chores to come in and help clean up.

"Well—it's understandable," my father said. "What she'd been through. And she had a little boy."

"Phip?"

"Hartley was always fond of kids."

"But if she was out of her mind, how could she look after him? Was she in one of those places? An asylum?"

"They came through it," my father said enigmatically, turning his attention to a cabinet leg he was chiselling on the lathe. "Your uncle doesn't say much about that time."

"Did you know Phip's real father was an artist?"

"Was he?" His attention was focused on removing the cabinet leg from the lathe and smoothing it with a fine sandpaper.

"He even drew naked people."

"Some artists do." Dad took the cabinet leg over to

the piece of wounded furniture he was repairing. "A pretty good fit, eh? There's two bits for you if you get the dust all cleaned up."

While I persisted questioning both of my parents, I never managed to get many more details from them. We saw Uncle Hartley and Phip from time to time over the next few years when they visited but I was shy around my uncle and I knew my mother wouldn't approve of me asking personal questions. Phip spent most of his time with Bradley at the hockey rink or on the ball diamond.

But even though there was no photograph of her out with the others in our living room, the image I had of the tall, scarred woman with her green glasses and fair hair remained clear in my mind. Everyone else was there on the bureau where Mom kept her best china, photos in elaborate wooden frames with inlaid patterns my father had created in his shop. Hartley, in his infantry uniform from World War I. Even as a young man, he was beefy and rather homely, but his wide smile was familiar. Phip, in his paratrooper uniform from the next war, was handsomer. He had light hair and good bone structure like his mother. There were photographs of Brad and me as babies and then a couple more as we grew. Grandparents now gone.

My mother and father had not been a young bride and groom. Their wedding picture was also on the bureau. Mom wore a matronly-looking rayon dress with cloth-covered buttons down the front that her mother had sewn, she told me, from a pattern they got from Eaton's catalogue. My father looked uncomfortable in a pin-striped suit, starched collar and paisley tie.

Uncle Hartley's and Aunt Harriet's wedding picture, though, was not there. I found it by chance one time as I rooted through a pile of old photos kept in the bureau's bottom drawer. In the photo, Uncle Hartley looked as if his dark hair had been glued to his head, a grooming manoeuvre that made his jaw and mouth seem even wider. The scars on Aunt Harriet's face had been smoothed out by the photographer. She wore no glasses and her eyes were nearly closed, giving her the appearance of someone close to swooning. She carried a bouquet of orchids. A small tiara crested her veil. I thought she was oddly beautiful in her long, shiny dress, pooling onto the studio carpet.

"Such expense," my mother commented when I brought out the photograph. "Dressed like a Russian princess and not being able to appreciate anything more than the feel of what she had on."

There were no other photographs of Aunt Harriet.

"I've been told she's camera shy," my mother said.

In 1950, when the brewing company Uncle Hart had worked for in the east opened a branch in Alberta, the family moved to Edmonton and Hartley's visits to Yarrow became more frequent—but Aunt Harriet never came with him.

Our kitchen, I had come to realize, had become my mother's territory of choice for heart-to-heart talks with Hartley when he visited. The coffee pot was an arm's reach from the drop-leaf table. Oilcloth spattered with a pattern of perpetual spring flowers seemed to encourage confidences. On any trip to Yarrow, Uncle Hartley would end up sooner or later across from my mother at this kitchen island.

When I was thirteen—almost fourteen—I remember one such visit. Uncle Hartley sitting stooped over his coffee. They had been discussing my grandmother's death a few years back and the topic settled heavily on both of them.

My mother sighed, refilled their coffee mugs and asked when Harriet might make the trip to Yarrow.

"She has something like a phobia about travelling. A short ride around town, you know. Out to dinner; out to a concert—that's about all she can manage."

"It's her loss," my mother had noted. "The air here in the country is a thousand times fresher, I'm sure, than it is in the city. And the trip from the city here, there's really so much to see ..."

Her sentence slipped away.

"You could tell ... describe ..."

"I do tell her. She always wants to hear all the details." Uncle Hart covered my mother's hand with his own at the table where they sat.

"You must miss the company," she said. "It's a pity Phip doesn't come with you more often."

"June keeps him on a fairly tight leash." Uncle Hartley's wide mouth stretched into a sad smile. Phip had recently married and, in fact, the last trip he'd made to Yarrow had been with his bride. She was a stylish-looking brunette with a phenomenal chest and tiny waist whom my mother immediately disliked. Bradley and I had been enchanted, though, following her every movement.

"Boobie heaven," Bradley had whispered in my ear from the hallway where we spied on the adult gathering in the living room. He pretended to have heart palpitations. Lately, Bradley had been ferreting home some of the pin-up magazines my father kept beneath the counter at his shop.

"June has her own notions," Uncle Hartley said.

My mother suddenly noticed me sitting in the little alcove in our kitchen between the cookstove and the cupboard, a place where I often hunkered down with a book, but equally often eavesdropped on adults at the kitchen table.

"Run outside and get some fresh air, Curtis," my mother said. "You need to build your muscles. Now, go."

A year earlier I had been bedridden with a bout of rheumatic fever and I had been cautioned, once recovery had been declared, to be careful about overexerting myself. In recent months, though, my mother fretted over my periods of inactivity, the hours I might spend sitting at a table with my drawing pad and pencil crayons, or lying on the sofa, reading my way through the novels of Frank Yerby and Frances Parkinson Keyes, steamy narratives that opened to me a past, romantic world and stirred me in ways that left me almost faint at times. It wasn't just the nature of my preoccupations that concerned her. I was passively rebellious, refusing to join the Boy Scouts or to be part of any sports team in which Bradley had shone.

"You don't want people to be calling you a sissy," she'd declared.

"I don't really care," I'd said. But it wasn't true. I did care, but even at thirteen—almost fourteen—I believed it was none of their business.

MY IDEA OF GETTING OUT IN THE FRESH AIR WAS TO walk from our house in the West End of town the few blocks that would take me to Main Street, a wide, gravelled thoroughfare. It was broad enough for most of the vehicles from the town and the farm area surrounding to nose into the sidewalks fronting Yarrow's few places of commerce—a small bank, a hotel with a false rectangular front, two grocery stores, a post office, a beauty parlour. Around the corner from my father's second-hand shop was the Municipal Building, which housed road-grading equipment in a barn-like garage. Attached to the garage was the tiny office of Yarrow's district commissionaire and an oblong meeting room that doubled as a public library.

Myron, the district commissionaire's son, kept the library hours faithfully, stoking the stove during the winter months, tending throughout the year to the checking out and returning of materials. A slow, affable man in his early thirties, he seemed to find great pleasure in setting the stamp each day and imprinting date due slips and borrower cards for the few patrons who straggled in to browse through a pitiful collection of primarily donated books.

"Myron was an accident," my mother had confided to me. "Jessie Evington thought she was going through the change of life and, in fact, it turned out she was pregnant with Myron."

I knew Myron's brothers were at least twenty years older than he was. One worked as our station agent; the other was a lawyer in Edmonton. As Myron put in his hours in the library, he laboured over a project which involved studiously recreating all the flags of the world on sheets from a jumbo writing pad, colouring the patterns in with crayons. He used an old reference book with an insert of global flags including such lost countries as Montenegro and Serbia.

He was intrigued when I brought my own drawing pad and looked enviously, I thought, at my collection of Laurentian pencil crayons boasting fifty-nine colours. Although Myron paid little attention to what the books were about that people borrowed, he soon realized that I drew people with something of the same dedication with which he tackled flags. He wandered by my table and giggled once as I meticulously copied the figure of Michelangelo's Adam reaching out to God from a reproduction in an ancient, donated set of encyclopedias. By the time I had reached the eighth grade, I had decided to become an artist and knew, from what I'd read or seen in films, that knowledge of human anatomy was something that would be expected of me. I was a willing researcher.

Remembering those years, from the onset of puberty until I was seventeen and packed my bags and left Yarrow to seek a university education, I think most of my waking—and many of my sleeping—moments were preoccupied with sex. When Bradley wasn't home, I would retrieve his stash of magazines from behind a beadwork kit containing a loom and a half-finished Indian headband at the back of his side of our closet, and flip through the pages, making myself dizzy with desire. Nudity in any form set my heart racing and sent blood rushing to my cheeks and other parts of my body. Bradley, catching me one day with his latest copy of *Playboy*, had taken it on himself to show me how to get relief, a revelation that amazed me.

"Just don't jerk off so Mom can tell. Use Kleenex and don't spill onto my magazines."

It was a mystery to me how male models might have posed for Michelangelo or Rodin without being in a perpetual state of tumescence.

Myron, with unexpected prescience, began to save aside any books he ran across containing pictures of the nude or near-nude: aged art history books, worn encyclopedias, donated copies of news magazines and the *National Geographic*. When I came into the library, if there was no one else present, he would bring these to me, always giggling as he opened them. In a way I was embarrassed by his knowledge of my interests, and, at the same time, I waited to see what he might have to show me and was disappointed if he had nothing set aside.

The Saturday Mom and Uncle Hartley had their kitchen visit, I sought the library to idle away a couple of hours. Myron beckoned me up into a small loft where he sorted through boxes and bags of donated books. Removing some German volumes from a box, he revealed several nudist magazines, naked men and women playing volleyball, climbing mountains, posing with bows and arrows, unabashedly sitting around campfires. I almost fell into the box, my eyes riveted to the profusion of sexual revelations, although for every handsome young man or girl, there seemed to be a horde of fairly overweight adults and paunchy seniors.

I was so preoccupied with the contents of this trove that it was a few minutes before I became aware that Myron had stopped giggling and his breathing had become laboured. When I checked to see what was happening, I realized he had undone his trousers and was massaging what seemed to me to be an incredibly long, engorged penis. As he climaxed, his free hand grasped my shoulder in something that I imagined to be almost a death grip. A shuddering gasp escaped into the dead air of the loft. I think, throughout all of this, I sat stock-still as a Rodin statue.

Myron cleaned himself with a handkerchief and said, haltingly, "Take them. For you."

The German nature-lover magazines were my secret companions for months, and I found myself thinking often of Myron Evington and his few small moments of ecstasy in the library loft. No one expected Myron to have a girlfriend, and, while I had a number of friends who were girls, I shied away from seeking one who might be steady in the way that Bonita, a girl in my class at school, had become Bradley's steady.

Of course, whenever Uncle Hartley visited, he would wag his shaggy eyebrows at me and ask me what little girl I was stepping out with.

"Curtis hasn't any time for romance," my mother said when her brother broached the subject on his last visit.

"Give him time, Hart. I don't think you had any girl-friends yourself before you went overseas."

I rarely entered into these conversations. They were really between the two of them, the kind of looping patter that adult siblings, to my continued astonishment, indulged in.

"When it comes to girls, I think he's shy like you always were. He'd sooner keep company with a book or a drawing pad." This led into a discussion about the family strands from which these predilections might be traced.

My mother remembered an aunt on the Martindale side of the family who painted on china.

"And our cousin Vernon," Uncle Hartley rubbed his chin thoughtfully. "Didn't he like to copy comic strip characters? Was pretty good at it. I remember he practically papered his room with them."

"So—artists on both sides," my mother decided.

They talked on until the coffee pot was empty and the sun was beginning to set.

"I'd better get going. Hat will think I had a car crash." Uncle Hartley pulled himself up from the kitchen chair with difficulty. He struggled to get his breath and gave me a little salute before heading out.

It was the last time we would see him.

CHAPTER 3

NEITHER BRADLEY NOR I ATTENDED OUR UNCLE Hartley's funeral, coming as it did when we were serving time at a church summer camp. I was not to see my Aunt Harriet until some six years after our Edmonton visit to the dentist. At that point in my life, I had settled into a basement room close to the U of A campus and sunk into the course work that would cough me out, a teacher, in two years time. Bradley was working at the Treasury Branch in Yarrow. He handed over a third of each paycheque to my mother, contributions to the family coffer that took on a concrete reality in new living-room wallpaper and a sofa set.

"Maybe, once you've got your certificate, you could get on at King George High," my mother mused. "It would be nice to have a chrome dinette for the kitchen."

I was being sponsored by the family for the two years it would take me to get my Standard S Certificate, she told me, and then "it was up to me." The phrase always hung in the air like some kind of suspension bridge. Somewhere at its other end it was secured by the prospect of my working at a school in Yarrow or at least within the district. Teaching English and art to the younger brothers and sisters of the kids I'd graduated with? It was a thought that filled me with unease. And, in fact, I was rather fond of the wooden drop-leaf table in our kitchen. Who knew what opportunities for escape the city might offer?

IT WAS DURING MY SECOND MONTH AS AN EDUCATION student, on a particularly dispiriting day filled with classes on Educational Psychology and The History of Education that I looked up Aunt Harriet's number in the phonebook. I wrote it on the inside cover of the scribbler I carried from class to class, its first few pages crammed with notes meandering through doodles and quick sketches. Over a cinnamon bun and coffee at the Tuck Shop, I flipped the cover open again, allowing a sprinkle of cinnamon to spill onto the name and the number so that I peered down on them as if through rust, the rust of all those years since I had seen her. What would happen if I called her? In my mind, I could see that strange, scarred face with its circles of bottle green glass, see her hands reaching for the telephone. Why would I want to call her? Where would it lead? A boy who always sat next to me in Sociology and was in the phys. ed. class I suffered through on a weekly basis crawled onto the vacant stool beside me and I closed the notebook quickly.

"Hi, Curtis."

"Walter." It was the first time I'd run into him outside of the classroom.

"Cramming away?" He was a large-boned, friendly boy with a shock of blond hair that looked to me like it had experienced a home-delivered peroxide treatment. "Double cinnamon buns." He winked at the waitress and held up two fingers.

We began comparing notes on our classes and instructors. As we talked, I felt an easing of the mood that had driven me to the telephone book. Homesickness, loneliness. Was this all it was? I walked with Walter over to the Reading Room of the library, crowded in the afternoon with students falling asleep into their books. We agreed to meet for supper at a small restaurant on Whyte Avenue where it was possible to eat without destroying our monthly budgets. On the honeyed varnish of the Reading Room table, I opened the scribbler again. It was more than loneliness or homesickness, I decided. There was curiosity there too, something that had never left me since that summer day we had visited the Coleman house. I wondered if the picture of the naked lady still hung in that small, dim parlour.

During an hour's break between classes the next day, I cornered the house phone in the Education Building and dialed the number. The voice of the woman who answered was familiar. The housekeeper who had met us at the door, I realized, must still be there. "Yes, she's in." There was that trace of an accent, perhaps a Scottish burr. "May I tell her who's callin'?"

As I waited, I rehearsed what I'd say to her. "You probably don't remember me. Surprise! Bet you probably never thought you'd hear from me. Remember your little nephews who visited you back in 1953?"

"Curtis." The voice was melodic, as deceptively youthful as it had been six years ago. "I was wondering when you'd give your old aunt a call."

"You knew I was in town?"

"Starting university?"

"Yeah. How'd you know?"

She laughed, the tinkly laugh I remembered. "I'm glad you're here," she said. "I've been missing male companionship."

"Isn't Phip around?"

"Phip's been back in Toronto for the past three years. Working for an advertising firm. He's remarried and comes to see me dutifully once a year. Here for three or four days and then gone again." There was a hesitation. "And how are your parents?"

The phone conversation settled comfortably into a familiar mode, friendly, expository. I chanted all the news I could think of, ending with details of where I had found room and board, what my university schedule was like. When I stopped for breath, she said, "You must come by soon so we can truly visit. How is Sunday?"

"Uh. Fine. Sunday would be fine."

"Dinner?"

I thought of the beetle.

"We'll eat out," she said with a slight laugh, as if she'd read my mind. "I don't get out enough. It'll give Jean a rest."

IT WAS A SUNDAY IN MID-OCTOBER, A WARM FALL DAY with a cloudless sky broken now and then with the distant, clamouring calls of migratory birds. In a blue blazer and grey flannels that had got me through graduation at King George High in Yarrow, I walked south of the university to the stucco bungalow where Bradley and I had fought over the doorbell. The house seemed smaller, the elm trees flanking it larger. Virtually all of the leaves had fallen and lay unraked across the lawn and walk.

Again, it was Jean Abercrombie who answered the door and I felt she had shrunk since I'd last seen her. She squinted up at my face.

"They should have tied a brick on you," she said wryly. "Your aunt's almost ready." She gestured me into the parlour. It was as I remembered, the walls filled with photographs, a few paintings and prints, the alcove with the small Tom Thomson oil and, among the chalk sketches there, yes—the naked lady. Jean Abercrombie exerted a gentle pressure against my arm and watched me fold into an armchair.

"I'll see if Harriet is ready for me to phone the taxi," she said, straightening an antimacassar I had dislodged in my descent.

Alone in the parlour, I tried to be impartial to the wall decorations, giving as much attention to the photograph of Uncle Hartley holding a trophy fish he'd caught, to Phip, caught by the camera in various stages of childhood and adolescence as I did the nude woman on the sofa, but finally I gave up and drank in every wondrous, re-affirming detail again. Was I getting a boner? Oh Christ, I thought. Who would believe this? The more I tried to pull my concentration from the sketch and what it was doing to me, the more my body became determined to acknowledge its sensuality. I crossed my legs and remained seated when Jean Abercrombie came back into the room. She looked at me oddly. "Your aunt's ready. I'll just go and call a cab now."

Then she was at the door. Aunt Harriet. She was much as I remembered her but her hair had gone white and she wore it in a coil on the back of her head. The circular dark glasses had been replaced with a style that had been recently popular, their flaring frames tipped with rhinestones. There were more rhinestones at her ears and neck.

"Curtis?" The voice was exploratory, her hands left the door frame for an instant, checking the fur jacket draped over her shoulders like a shawl, the black velvet dress, a beaded handbag.

"Aunt Harriet." It was safe to stand.

She bore the weight of a person who has been sedentary for many years but I was surprised by her long legs, her large feet in black patent slippers. A "Scandahoovian" I remembered now my mother had once described her. "Feet and hands like a lumberjack."

"Come here and give me a hug."

I came from a family of non-huggers. Goodnight kisses and impromptu hugs had stopped once I was old enough to attend school. Once in a while, at Christmas or on a birthday, we hugged one another, but always quickly and clumsily, like people at a rehearsal before they've got things right. I moved awkwardly to Aunt Harriet and wrapped my gangly arms around her fur-covered shoulders. There was a smell in the old, shedding skins of her jacket that made me think of our attic in Yarrow and the musty boxes of clothing goods I sometimes sorted through in my father's second-hand shop. In that brief hug, I caught too the aroma of a perfume, a floral attar with a hint of lilacs to it. And face powder. Like my mother's.

I felt her own arms go around me, pulling me close. "You've become very tall and thin," she said, releasing me. Before I had a chance to step away, though, a hand lit gently on my face, fingertips tracing my brow, my cheekbones, brushing along my nose, my lips and chin. "Do you mind?"

"No." I stood patiently.

"Are you handsome?" She smiled, the lipsticked rim of her lips suddenly impish.

"I wish I were," I laughed. "Bradley got the looks."

"Well, it doesn't matter so much if you're thin." She patted my arm. Gesturing to me to return to my seat, she made her way to that same armchair where I had first been introduced to her. "Would you believe I was very slender at your age?" she said, her fingers searching the table for the carved box of cigarettes. I watched her complete the intricate task of lighting up. She drew in smoke and held it as if she were giving it an opportunity to visit all parts of her interior self. "Yes, I was thin and, I think, handsome. When you get to be my age you can say such things. Handsome rather than pretty. That figure study of me errs on the side of softness and femininity." She gestured vaguely over her shoulder to the nude on the sofa hanging among the other sketches in the alcove.

"It was you?"

"Was?"

"I was remembering when we came to visit you when Brad and I were kids. I guessed then that it was you. Mom was a bit upset. She'd never seen a naked lady on a living-room wall before."

Aunt Harriet exhaled a small chuckle with a wisp of smoke. "I have it there on purpose," she said. "It helps me to figure people out. You need some small subterfuges when one of your senses is gone. Of course, I didn't have anything on the walls for a long time—until after the war, I think—in Toronto. Jean hung some ornaments and Hartley had a few photographs around but then, in 1946, when Phip was going back to college and studying to become a commercial artist, he asked if he could look through his father's sketches. A few that were the least damaged he had trimmed and framed. I think he always wanted to say to visitors, 'The naked lady is actually a portrait of my mother,' but he never quite got up the courage. When we moved to Edmonton, he arranged everything as close as possible to how it was back east."

"Do you have any of the artwork Phip has done?"

"No. Sometimes he'd describe a piece he was working on to me. But I could never keep the pictures in my mind the way I could those of Phillip's that I had actually seen, looked at over and over again. I think he had some of his paintings up—mainly in his bedroom—but after

Hartley died he took all of his stuff with him when he left June and moved back to Toronto."

Her cigarette had burned down and she carefully snuffed it out in the glass tray. "Of course, I've always had the Thomson up. I like to feel it as I walk by."

Jean appeared at the doorway, dressed now, herself, for going out. "The taxi's here. If you don't mind, I'll tag along to my bus connection." She carried a stack of magazines to donate to the hospital where her diabetic sister, she told me in some detail, was recovering from an amputation.

After we had let her out, Harriet sighed and said, "We are of an age when parts of us must be lost. Jean was in the hospital herself a year ago for two months. Some doctor taking out a good portion of her inner workings. I hired a university student for the time she was gone. That was an unqualified disaster."

"How long has Jean been with you?" The cab was onto the High Level Bridge and its grillwork fell in patterns of shadow across us.

"Since she was a young woman. Since we were both young women." The repeating intervals of shadow seemed, I thought, to mark time, its quick, regular flight. "She was the housekeeper when Phip was born." I felt her hand grasp mine. "Curtis, I'm so glad you've come," she said. "I've been waiting."

I didn't know what to say so I cleared my throat and, seeing her struggle with a package of cigarettes in her handbag, offered to light one for her. She smoked in silence as the cab eased its way from light to light along Jasper Avenue, drawing up finally to the MacDonald

Hotel. "We may discover some new cafés," she told me, almost conspiratorially, "but I thought we should start with something sure."

I had never before eaten at a restaurant with cloth napkins and candlelight playing off heavy silver cutlery. Aunt Harriet's rhinestones wakened, glinting as she nodded at the waiter, ordering wine. "Hartley liked to come here," she said matter-of-factly. "For special occasions, you know."

Bringing the wine, the waiter reviewed the menu. I mumbled assent to Aunt Harriet's choices and we settled down over the claret. In my experience, red wine was sweet and fruity, stuff my father bought by the jug. The MacDonald Hotel claret caught in my throat.

"How do you like the wine?" Aunt Harriet seemed to be playing with it in her mouth. "You must be looking very sophisticated. They didn't ask to see your birth certificate."

"It's not very sweet."

"I should hope not," she laughed. Again her hand found mine. "Bear with your old aunt," she said. I took another mouthful. "So you're going to be a teacher. What happened to the writing and the drawing?"

"Oh, I still do those." The verb "do" seemed suddenly silly. "I'm still interested."

"Are you working on anything at the moment?"

"Not really." The claret was going down more easily. "I'm taking an art option and I just write when I have a chance. Not very often since courses started."

"Do you keep a journal, Curtis?" The question, I felt, had more import than the words put to me.

"No," I admitted.

She released my hand and sank back in her chair.

"Phillip Pariston did," she said, her voice soft and distant. "For almost a year."

"I should keep one," I laughed. "But nothing interesting's happened to me yet. Nothing heroic." She urged me to tell her about the unheroic episodes of my first few weeks in the city. Through the salad and the chicken cordon bleu, I entertained her with an account of finding a room, after a gruelling search, in a building with a caretaker who would have been snapped up by Roger Corman for one of his horror movies if Edmonton had been Hollywood. I followed this up with a blow-by-blow description of registration, a scenario that I dubbed "Curtis Hayseed tackles the Big U." She laughed politely, at times maybe even with genuine mirth.

"Do you care for music?" she asked me over coffee. I was struck by how our conversation throughout the evening took on the texture of a boy and girl out on a first date, or what I imagined a date would be like if I ever had one.

"Uh, sure," I answered. "But I don't know much about classical."

"It's like claret," she said. "You can develop a taste for it."

She was growing tired, I could see, and she gave me her purse to sort out the dinner bill and pay the taxi home. As we drew up in front of her house, though, she insisted I come in. Jean had returned and fussed over us at the door. I made a much-needed trip to the bathroom. Except for the pictures and furnishings in the parlour, there was little

I could see of my aunt's influence in the rest of the house. A doll with a crocheted skirt hiding a spare roll of toilet paper stared fixedly at me as I came to terms with two hours of claret and coffee. Plaster seahorses frolicked on a deep turquoise wall. In the hallway, an embossed mirror separated some India ink silhouettes of Scottie dogs and a trio of sun-bleached Maxfield Parrish posters.

When I returned to the parlour, Jean was lowering the phonograph needle onto an LP. A plaintive violin solo filled the room.

"I once played this for the Vancouver Women's Musical Society," Aunt Harriet informed me. The violin was news to me, a piece missing from the family gossip. What would my mother have done with that?

"After Phillip died, I rarely played again. At times for parties in the boarding house. Helped pay for my keep. But that wasn't Brahms. Dance music I could play by ear." She was sipping something the colour of fire and gold from a large snifter. "Cocoa is on the way. Jean says I am not to offer you brandy. She disapproves of me having it myself. I can remember a time, though, when she liked her own little tumbler of whiskey at the end of the day."

We listened, without talking, as the violin explored the evening, hovering over the dim lamplight which softened the contours of the naked lady on the sofa, allowed the indigos and blackish-greens of the Thomson to recede even farther into their lakeshore landscape, muted the photographs to quiet, frozen ghosts. At times the music picked up and rippled through the swirls of Aunt Harriet's cigarette smoke. I thought I saw moisture along the cross-hatching of scars on her face. "If only ..." she muttered.

I waited for her to finish her sentence but the violin solo faded into silence and, in the pause between selections, she called out for Jean to bring her the symphony schedule. "Do you mind," she said, "going with me? Jean hates them."

CHAPTER 4

"**S**O—WHAT DO YOU THINK?" AUNT HARRIET asked me as we settled into another MacDonald Hotel supper following the symphony a few weeks later.

"I've already acquired a taste," I said. "'Greensleeves' was wonderful. And the piano in that Franz Liszt piece. I'm not sure about the opera singer."

"We won't ask for everything all at once." Aunt Harriet smiled. "A coloratura singing 'The Laughing Song' is perhaps too much by way of an initiation."

The outing had given both of us an appetite, and it seemed that neither of us drew breath until we had devoured our servings of prime rib.

"Music brought us together," Aunt Harriet said, over the last bits of apple tart we ordered for dessert. "Phillip and me." She searched for a napkin that had fallen to the floor.

"I'll get it."

"If Edwina had only known ..." A chuckle, like the sound of some small summer insect surfaced, retreated.

"Edwina?"

"Phillip's stepmother. I know she rued the day she ever brought us together but it was Edwina who led to the two of us meeting. One of her evening musicales. Putting on the dog for Vancouver society. Fruit punch and petits fours. Madame Avocasti singing Massenet and Faure. If you thought the coloratura was a trial this afternoon, you should have heard Madame Avocasti. Phillip was on the piano—he wasn't very good either, but the pieces were difficult. I was someone she had discovered who was willing to play during the evening for a modest fee. I was nineteen and he was twenty. Oh my, we were so young ..." Aunt Harriet drew a cigarette out of her cigarette case and held it expectantly between her long fingers. I touched her other hand to let her know I was ready with a match and she put the cigarette to her lips, drawing smoke in and keeping it there the way a swimmer might hold onto oxygen during a plunge into depths.

"So young," she said, releasing the smoke. "He walked me home." She felt for an ashtray. "To Cordova Street down on the waterfront where Papa and I had a small flat. I didn't ask him in—I could see Papa was home—but he kissed me goodnight and offered to come to the store and pick me up when I was finished work the next day. Talk about being smitten, Curtis, but then he was incredibly good-looking and so ... what? Gallant. I know it's not a word that's used any more but it fits Phillip somehow."

For those who have become blind rather than being born blind, I suspected there must be a repertoire of images to which the mind turns and returns. Was the image of Phillip Pariston in Aunt Harriet's consciousness sharpened and constantly refocused by the blackness of elapsed years? As she sat, as still as the evening itself, I sensed she was searching for some way to present what she saw to me, to bring me in with her somehow to that constantly revisited interior.

"In a way," she said, "he was shy about the impression he made. People would sometimes just stop and stare at him, the way you might if you saw an exquisite plant in bloom, or a sleek and graceful animal. It made him blush."

"It's not a problem I've ever had," I admitted.

A trace of a smile crossed Aunt Harriet's lips. "His brother Everett always said Phillip got the looks for both of them. Not that Everett was homely, but he always insisted his ears were too big. Actually he looked pretty good in uniform."

"He joined up but Phillip didn't?"

"Oh—Phillip tried. It was the thing to do, of course, but I think he was rather relieved when he was turned down. He thought he could maybe sign on as a war artist once he became accomplished enough."

"He wasn't well?"

Aunt Harriet, I could see, had retreated once again to her images and I felt my prompting was lost in some preoccupation of her own, my words like moths beating against the incandescence of a lamp. But she surprised me a couple of minutes later.

"Rheumatic fever," she said. "He had it as a child and there was some ..." she paused, searching out a word hidden in the corners of her memory, "irregularity. He had an irregular heartbeat."

She must have heard my small gasp.

"What?" She carefully extinguished her cigarette and reached for my hand.

"Oh, nothing," I said. "It's just so odd. It's true of me too. The irregular heartbeat. And I spent a few months in bed with rheumatic fever when I was thirteen."

"Parallel lives," Aunt Harriet said. "There are so many things that are true of the two of you. Do you believe in fate?"

At that point in my life I believed in very little. "Fate?" My voice fluttered.

"An order, a scheme that brings us to points of intersection. I catch glimpses of it although sometimes the intersections are almost beyond bearing."

A silence settled over the taxi ride back across the river to Aunt Harriet's house. As we went in and I helped her with her wrap, she grasped my hand.

"I have something to show you," she said.

I found myself focusing on the word "show" the way I often did when she used any words involving sight.

"Phillip's papers." She eased herself into her armchair. "It's time you two met. Jean always leaves them in a box beneath the sideboard."

It was the kind of cardboard box used by Eaton's for gift-wrapping garments. I folded back the top. An encased book, secured with a clasp, nested in a pile of sketches, fragments that I could see, at a quick glance, held images in pencil and charcoal. Some offered the muted hues of chalk and watercolour. Most of the papers were torn or partially burned and some were spotted with dots and smudges of oil.

"The journal should be on top," Aunt Harriet indicated.

"Yes. It's here."

"Why don't you read me the first entry?"

The cover was a maroon that had probably darkened over the decades, a fine-tooled leather in good condition except for one burned corner. Inside it had marbled end-papers and cardboard pockets with photographs, clip-pings, and letters tucked in them. My fingers brushed against the uneven edge of this assemblage before moving to turn the first page. The heavy cream paper had buckled from dampness at some point but, while some of the words had become bleached and fuzzy, the damage was patchy and none of what I saw was illegible.

November 18, 1916, I read, *Today was my birthday, but really Old Grand's evening, and—with the gift of this book—it seems fitting that he should be the subject of its first sentence.*

"With all you do on paper," he said, "you may think it fool-ish to keep a record of what's happening in your young life, but it's something I wish I had done when I was your age."

We were having coffee at the Delmonico following the Carnegie Library lecture. By that time I had unwrapped the curious package he had been carrying along with him through-out the evening.

"Imagine you are writing it to be read by yourself at my age," he added.

"And make it sound like a Thackeray novel?"

He chuckled. "Something like that. But who shall you be? Henry Esmond? Not Barry Lyndon, I hope."

And so I begin this journal. The fountain pen came with it. I suspect Old Grand thought I would be easily seduced by the ease with which it yields its ink (black—it seems nothing can be hidden from you, wise old man—you know my fondness for black) and the broad cut of the nib which encourages calligraphic flourishes. I have already made an elaborate design on the blotter.

The journal, it turns out, is only a small part of Grand's gift. He has offered to set me up with a stipend so I can go to the States or perhaps to Toronto to pursue my studies in painting. I'm afraid I was shamefaced over his generosity when I considered all of the hinting I have done toward this end. But then, of course, my thoughts flew to Harriet. As if he could read my mind, Old Grand said that, as a student, it would be important for me to remain "unencumbered."

"You like Harriet," I countered.

"I love her dearly," Old Grand said, "but waiting a year or two until you become more established ..."

It was all I could do not to accuse him of caving in to Edwina and Dads, who must have been at him about all this.

"Give it some thought," he said, so gently that I could not find it in my heart to rail at him. "Now, let's walk—I want to stroll along the beach."

He walks less quickly these days, Old Grand. We stopped often—once even for him to light and smoke part of a cigar.

"I'm glad you're out of this foolishness." He stood looking out to sea, as if he might somehow penetrate its great expanse and see to the other side of the world, even past Mongolia to Russia and Europe where the war rages. "I worry about your brother. He's never had any sense of caution."

I had to agree with him as I thought of Everett balancing high on a railing of the Connaught Bridge or diving off Dads' boat into water all of us thought too turbulent for swimming.

The result of our long ramble is that it is too late now to slip over to Hat's. If I remember correctly, it is Ahlstrom's day off and I have no particular desire to encounter Hat's father — especially when he has been drinking throughout the evening.

It was bad enough to encounter Edwina parked in the green parlour when we came in. I think, over the afternoon and evening, she'd managed to down a decanter of brandy. By the time she got up from the chaise and made her way to the entranceway, Old Grand had already made his escape. Which left me trying to make sense of what she was saying. She seems to be in a tizzy over the musical evening she has planned for next week. I guess the violinist was called up and has left a big gap in the program.

"I can check to see if Hat is free that night," I said. As usual when I mentioned Hat's name, Edwina's eyes glazed over.

"There should be an exemption for musicians," she said, patting my arm in that kind of absent way she has at times. "I'm sure they're no good at fighting, and they're so — needed. Needed on the home front." Then she became teary-eyed again over last week's listings and the death of Robbie Beaton.

I must say it saddened me too, even if Robbie was, at times, painful to be around. He did play a sweet clarinet. I'll give him that.

PHILLIP'S VOICE, I REALIZED, RODE EASILY ON MY OWN.
When I'd finished the passage, Aunt Harriet sighed and
there followed one of those silences to which I was to
become accustomed, silences defined by the soft mechanical insistence of a parlour clock, and the muted music of
the phonograph, the scattering of lamplight when it hit her
brandy glass or danced away from the rhinestones on her
glasses. In the silences I felt she must retreat into remembered worlds for small ruminative visits. Often she would
oar back to the present with a sudden word or phrase.

"'The Piccadilly Pigeon.' That's what Phillip used to
call Edwina. Not to her face of course. But she was a bit of
a snob, Edwina, and wasn't anxious to remind people that
she'd had her day on the stage."

"She'd been an actress?"

"That would be stretching it. She sang in music
halls. I think 'The Canary of Covent Garden' was what
they might actually have called her. Phillip kept invent-
ing other names for her. 'The Chelsea Chipper.' 'The
Piccadilly Pigeon.'" Aunt Harriet laughed softly. "I think
Phillip's father met her when she was in some show or
other, although why he ever married her was, I am sure,
an eternal mystery to the family."

"How did Phillip get along with her?"

"Phillip was a peacemaker, I guess you might say.
Everett, I was to discover, had much less patience with
her, and he was an incorrigible tease. He would bait her.
But Phillip—he would tear his hair out at times—but
he wasn't unkind. For his father's sake, I think, he was
always indulgent to Edwina."

Aunt Harriet sank deeper into her chair and let another small silence collect around her. "I wish he had come over," she said. "It's odd how the details of some days can stay with you while, in other instances, months—even years—can slip away. The evening seemed three times as long as it ever was. I remember sewing a bit, and I practiced a Brahms piece, but it was difficult to focus. I kept going to the window. There was a fine rain falling. From my third-storey bedroom I could look down on the people passing, dock workers headed home, men going to their rooms for a beer.

"I knew he'd been out with his grandfather for a special birthday evening and I had a kind of foreboding about it all. When Phillip was with me, I felt that nothing could separate us, but when he was away from me, I was quickly filled with uncertainty. I knew his family wished I would just disappear from his life. I think I imagined everything in the world—everything from the two of us running off and being secretly married to my being abandoned with a child."

A small, bitter laugh punctuated this observation and Aunt Harriet extended her now empty brandy snifter toward me. "Just a small drop," she said.

The last Brahms waltz on the record faded and I changed it for an LP of a Schubert sonata, the violin music edging around us with its own variations on boldness and uncertainty.

"I had it in my mind that if he came over to see me, however late, that everything would be right with the world. You know, those kinds of games we play with our minds from time to time. If a sailboat passes the protruding edge of the seawall before the streetlamps come on ... I watched out the window, thinking time and again that I could see him rounding the corner onto Cordova and hurrying along the block, but it was always someone else and then, finally, I did see Papa coming home, walking in a way that left no doubt in my mind where he'd been for the evening.

"I knew he'd be angry. My father was not a mellow drunk. He would come home raging, raging against his boss, raging at the conditions on his dock job, raging against what life had done to bring him to a cramped cold-water flat on Cordova Street, with a daughter to raise and no wife to help. Raging because he thought people had looked down their noses at him in a restaurant or as he walked along the street. Sometimes I think he couldn't even focus his anger—he was just simply angry. It was a good thing our Lithuanian landlady was half in love with him or we likely wouldn't have had a place to stay. He was a handsome man, I must say, Curtis, even if he was rough and, when he'd been drinking, rowdy."

Jean came in and made a gesture towards her wrist-watch for my benefit. Spookily, it seemed that Aunt Harriet had divined exactly what she'd done.

"Don't be a mother hen," she chided.

"Did your father...?" My voice failed to complete the sentence but she gathered my intent and waved her left hand dismissively.

"He never beat me."

Jean hovered in the doorway. "Some folk can stay up to the wee small ..." she grumbled good-naturedly, "but I'm off for my beauty sleep."

I eased one of the old photographs from its cardboard pocket. It was a grouping of four men. The Pariston men, I assumed.

"I remember hiding away the gift I had waiting for Phillip. Some piano pieces he'd been wanting. I had rolled them and tied them with ribbon interwoven with a lock of my hair. I put the coffee on—sometimes I could tame Per with a few cups of coffee. When he came in he saw I'd been crying and I had a time convincing him no one had hurt me, that I just wasn't feeling well."

THE SUBJECT OF PER CAME UP A FEW WEEKS LATER when, once again, I'd settled into an evening of music and remembrance following a concert and supper at the Blue Willow downtown. I'd read another passage from the journal, Phillip recounting an awkward encounter with Per on Pender Street, Harriet's father bowing elaborately to him and doffing his hat in front of a group of his steve-dore buddies.

"Tell me about him," I said.

She did. And years later, when I had begun to tape her stories so that I would never lose them, I had her tell me again.

"Per?" Her voice emerges from the slowly moving wheels of the tape recorder. "I think Per was one of those people who always wanted things to be better than they were but who could never quite manage to figure out how to do it—or, if he did figure it out, would as quickly sabotage the effort. I suppose it's what, today, they call a feature of the classic alcoholic—someone who is adept at not succeeding. I did love him, though, Curtis. It was a tough corner of the world—the waterfront back in those days before and during the war. I remember heading off to school and there would be men, a line that seemed to stretch forever, assembled along the street in front of the Auxiliary Hall and often Papa would be in the lineup and he'd wave or I'd hear him call out, '*Farvel, skjaere!* Bye bye little magpie.' I always thought the men looked exhausted—I guess, in a way, it was wearying to their souls to line up day after day, never certain you'd be picked and make the money you'd need to get through the week or a month.

"There would be times when Per would get in with one of the gangs—often they were looking for experienced longshoremen to unload and load the Empress boats or the Australian line. I think if a foreman got to know you and saw you as a good worker, you would have regular work. I remember for a while he was part of the sugar gang and he hated that, loading two-hundred-and-forty-pound sacks of sugar. In the lower holds, the sacks would get stuck together and it took almost superhuman strength to get them apart and stacked just the way a foreman wanted them."

There is a pause and the sound of a brandy glass being replenished.

In my mind's eye, I can see Aunt Harriet raising the snifter and taking a small sip.

"Per was strong. He'd been working on boats or on the docks all his life. But he'd never kept a regular job for long. I think he often felt he knew better than the foreman how to load a ship's hold and then there'd be a scrap and he'd be back standing in the drizzle outside the hall. If he'd been drinking, the scraps would get physical and there'd be months when it was hard for him to get any work at all. Those were lean times, let me tell you. I was lucky if I had a couple of slices of bread with a bit of syrup sticking them together for lunch.

"Sometimes he'd work a boat which would load up at the docks and then he'd go with it for the unloading. I'd be on my own for a few days—which I never minded, even when I was twelve or thirteen. I remember once—oh my!—he got into such a state. He loaded a ship with rails for Squamish and I think it was going up to Ocean Falls too and the longshoremen were asked to go along to unload. I guess the only accommodation they had for them was the straw on the poop deck and there were three pigs corralled there. They had to bed down with the pigs for several days.

"'*Gris. Svinepels!*' he would be roaring when he had a few under his belt. 'We might as well be pigs!'"

I recall a smile flickering across Aunt Harriet's lips.

"Poor Papa. He was such a mixture of things. Angry so much of the time. And always drinking too much. But he played the violin as if the music were part of his blood. Nothing classical. He'd pretty well taught himself although I think his own father was supposed to have been a pretty good fiddler.

"Your mother? Was she with you?"

"Mama." The word was as soft as a whisper on Aunt Harriet's lips. "She died when I was nine. In Seattle. That was when Papa and I came up to Vancouver. I think he couldn't bear living in a place so filled with memories."

The words spill into a stretch of silence.

But that autumn evening in 1959 there was the sound of Aunt Harriet's parlour clock chiming midnight.

"Heavenly days," she laughed, "where has the evening flown!"

I remember returning the journal to its nest of paper fragments, resisting for the moment the urge to pull them out and scrutinize them more closely. There would be other evenings, I knew.

IN THE COMING MONTHS IT WAS A ROUTINE I GREW TO love, reading Phillip Pariston's diary aloud to Aunt Harriet in the evenings after we had been to a concert or supper.

Often I thought of my mother's disclosure that Harriet had been—what?—mentally unstable?—surely not insane. I was reluctant to ask about the horrors of that distant time. But one December evening, after we'd been for dinner and the symphony, I saw a side that was new.

"Perhaps we shouldn't have gone."

I had filled her brandy glass, generously, from the decanter on the sideboard. Jean was out for the evening and she had left a plate of fruitcake pieces, covered with a Christmas napkin.

"You're tired?" I pressed the plate toward her. "Fruitcake."

"No." She batted it away. "I hate fruitcake. I'm surprised Jean can't remember." A few of the pieces fell into my lap. As I retrieved them, she took a swallow of brandy that made her choke.

"Some music ... the Rubenstein ..." She gasped and some of the brandy spilled from her snifter. "It is in my mind like a piece of glass that has never been picked out."

"Was it...?"

"I thought I might want to hear it again." She took another swallow and closed her eyes as if the constant darkness needed another curtain. "But some things can never fit ... back ... the way they should."

I had no idea what to say.

Suddenly she laughed.

"Paste it all together. Sound and shatter ... what we want to be ... what is." She tipped the brandy glass to her lips. "Oh look, I must have spilled some." Laughing, she held it out.

As I was refilling it, Jean returned, coming in the front door with a gust of wind.

"The cold is settling," she said, divesting herself of coat and boots. It was an expression that was uniquely hers, as if weather came like a surge of immigrants.

I expected her to go on about her evening at a church dinner but whatever she was poised to say turned to silence. She was looking at Harriet with concern. Maybe because Harriet had continued laughing, a quiet laugh but one that scattered around the room as she twisted in her chair. She hurried over and laid her hands on Harriet's shoulders.

"No." The laugh turned into an almost inaudible moan. Then louder and sustained. "No."

Jean looked at me. "You'll be wanting to get home before it gets any colder." She was rubbing her hands soothingly along Aunt Harriet's arms now in what struck me as something she might have done often even though I had never seen her do it before.

I nodded and retrieved my own winter gear.

"Goodnight," I said.

Her answer was barely a whisper.

"Goodnight, Phillip."

CHAPTER 5

EVEN WITH AUNT HARRIET'S FRIENDSHIP, MOST OF that first year at university, I was lonely. I think I had hopes that the shyness that had wrapped me like some kind of invisible cloak in Yarrow would fall away in this new setting, in the big city. I had a little money from a bursary I had accepted and not told my mother about since it entailed teaching for two years for Edmonton Public Schools and I knew she wanted me to settle back home. With the bursary augmenting my allowance, I had funds enough to consider going out on dates. But I had never dated in Yarrow—never really dated. I'd gone to the local dances with friends and the girls I knew enjoyed dancing with me—I was a good dancer—but I was always just the guy pal, a designation I wore with the same comfort as my dancing shoes.

That fall I worked up the courage to ask out a girl who often set up her easel beside me in our drawing lab. During breaks we slipped out for coffees together. I enjoyed her wicked sense of humour. She could describe our regular, flabby female model, Mrs. Hyde-Bennett, in terms that left me weak with laughter. But when I finally got the nerve to ask her to go to a movie with me, she gave me a quick smile and said sure but I should know she was dating one of her professors. She couldn't say who that was but she was sure he wouldn't mind if she went out with me. It was the kind of "me" that translated as "brother" or "good friend." I felt that wave of embarrassment I always got when I sensed any kind of rejection. "Sure, let's do that," I said with practiced nonchalance. But we never did.

I did take time out from my studies to catch a movie or grab a bite at one of the South Side diners. Quite often by myself, but other times Walter Mandriuk would catch up with me and come along. I knew he watched for me when he was in the Tuck Shop. We ran into each other too in Sociology, a huge, massed class hosted in the Agriculture Building auditorium since the Education Building was bursting at its seams with baby boomers determined to become teachers.

First-year Education students were obliged to take phys. ed. and Walter and I ended up taking the course in the same time slot. He was a phys. ed. major, though, while I was someone who dragged myself reluctantly to the soccer field and the gym. Aware of how unathletic, pale, and skinny I appeared in the buff, I quickly changed into regulation gym shorts and jerseys but, when we were finished, avoided the shower room adjacent to our lockers. Walter and most of the others in my class bounded back and forth in unabashed displays of nudity. There were times when the mixture of steam and testosterone brought me close to dizziness. I tried to convince myself that I was viewing it all with the eyes of an artist making notes about male anatomy. My glances were quick and furtive. Usually my getaways from the locker room were executed with the speed of lightning.

Walter would catch me hurrying into my clothes, grabbing my books, ready to sprint to my next class.

"Not showering today, Curt?"

"Naw. No time to get dry. I just have ten minutes to get to English all the way across campus."

"Dinner tonight at the cafeteria?"

"Uh ... sure."

"Meet you there at six."

There was an ease to Walter that I admired. He seemed comfortable within his skin, always a ready smile on his lips, strong straight teeth, large farm-boy hands that every once in a while strayed to my arm as we sat and ate, emphasizing the punchline of a joke or reinforcing some bit of irony he discovered in campus life. In some ways, he was fearless in what he said.

"Cocks." One of those first dinners we shared, the word dangled like the piece of spaghetti that had escaped onto his chin, making him laugh.

"What!"

"Cocks. I think all of those cocks in the locker room scare you away." He winked at me. It was something else he could do effortlessly, and I had never been able to do at all. Wink. "You never even get out of your underwear."

"I don't know what you're talking about."

"Penises," he said. "And all the equipment that goes with them. If you happen to be sitting on a locker room bench, you practically get hit in the eye. You never stick around though."

I could feel red creeping up my face to my hairline and I looked around to see if anyone was sitting close enough to be listening in.

"There, I made you blush." Walter showed all of his front teeth when he laughed.

"I don't know how you got started on this," I sputtered. "I told you, I have to run like Pheidippides to get to class after phys. ed. Whereas you can spend ten minutes in a hot shower."

"Right." Walter tried to look contrite, but I could see a smile still playing along his lips.

We were both coffee addicts so we met quite often at the Tuck Shop and sometimes at my basement apartment where I'd lined the walls with paintings and sketches from the art course I was taking. He liked checking out what he called my "gallery" and he knew I could always rustle up a snack. While there was no stove in my apartment, there was a cupboard and a sink and enough counter space for an electric hot plate. The rest of the furnishings were from my father's second-hand store, trucked into Edmonton by a friend of his—a small wooden table and a couple of mismatched chairs he'd sanded and stained with a honey-coloured varnish, and a Winnipeg couch that I could use as a sofa during the day and unfold into a bed at night.

"What's new in the gallery?" Walter would ask, inspecting whatever new pieces I'd tacked up onto the beaverboard walls. "Do they ever hire good-looking models?"

"No," I laughed. "I think it's a requirement that the women are overweight and have varicose veins and stretch marks. Men have to be at least over fifty, generally as skinny as the women are fat."

"And they wear jockstraps?"

"Some anatomical secrets need to be kept when it comes to males."

"No secrets in the phys. ed. building locker room," Walter noted.

I gave him a look. We were not going to get into that conversation again.

"Were you pathologically shy as a child?" Walter asked me one time when he'd followed me home. I'd promised to grill us a cheese sandwich and brew some coffee.

"Not pathologically," I said.

"But shy."

"I come from a family where we kept our clothes on. Well, of course, Bradley and I ..."

"Bradley?"

"My brother."

"Ah."

He shook his head and smiled at me. When he reached over and put his hand on mine, though, I jerked away, more of a reflex than anything else. I thought I saw a flicker of fear—or was it anger?—in his eyes, but then he laughed.

"You are your own funny self," he said. "But don't change."

We still got together for the odd meal and once, when Aunt Harriet was fighting a cold and didn't feel like going, Walter went with me to a concert at the Jubilee Auditorium. Mendelssohn at his most mellow.

After the performance, we found a coffee shop on 109th Street.

"So this is part of that other world of yours," he said, checking out the couples and small groups at tables dimly lit with candles caught in coloured glass and fish netting.

"The music, yes," I said. "The smoke-filled restaurant, no."

"I'm glad," he chuckled. "I think I could get to like the music."

CHAPTER 6

THE SUMMERS BETWEEN UNIVERSITY TERMS I returned to Yarrow to help in my father's second-hand shop. It was a slow business at the best of times, so my presence at the counter served more to give him time during the day to catch a few hours of fishing or have a drink with his cronies in the beer parlour of the small stucco-covered hotel which anchored the other end of Main Street. Because the bank manager at the Treasury Branch was on the United Church Board, Bradley, for July and August both years, managed to escape town to work as a counselor and lifeguard at the church camp on Garrett Lake.

"You could get on as a crafts teacher and take the Bible study," my mother had urged.

"I may not be of legal age yet," I told her, "but if you force me to work at the camp, I'll run away and join a circus ... or take up drug-running."

"Think of the good you'd be doing. I know they're short ..."

I recalled my summer internments at Garrett Lake throughout my teens, and shuddered. "Besides," I said, "I've become an agnostic."

"When did you join them?" She looked sharply at me. "I don't think Mr. Burcock would mind. He had that Cherkowski girl working there last summer and her parents are Greek Orthodox."

I shot my father a pleading look.

"Let him work at the shop, Violet," he said. "He's good at tidying things."

So I tidied for a couple of hours each day, sorting through boxes of odds and ends that lined the rear of the shop, giving it a strange, bunkered appearance—a wall of cardboard, out of which poked bits of clothing and footwear, edges of magazines, kitchenware and discarded machinery. My mission was to get the contents of the boxes into their appropriate plywood bins and containers that my father had attached to the other walls. From the woodworking corner of the shop there was a nest of shavings which I swept up each day. Sawdust settled like fine sandy ash over everything when he worked with the saws, so keeping that at bay was another ongoing task, one that he happily relinquished to me.

In actuality, sorting, sweeping, dusting, and waiting on customers took only a chunk of each day and I filled my free time reading novels from the shelves of used paperbacks by the front door, sketching from my *Anatomy for Artists* textbook, and writing letters to Aunt Harriet. I could imagine Jean reading them to her in the parlour with the drapes drawn for coolness. In my mind, I could see her lips, on the verge of breaking into a smile, perhaps even laughter. In turn, she would dictate brief notes—Jean was not a patient scribe—outlining her own sparse summer activities, the books she was reading, her thoughts about the music she listened to on records or the radio.

Conspiratorially, I collected the mail each day from the post office two doors down from the second-hand shop. Why I didn't want my mother to know that Aunt Harriet and I exchanged letters I am uncertain. I suspect it was because the small rebelliousness and paranoia of my adolescence was not far behind me and I had grown into habits of furtiveness.

I never thought about it at the time but I think my inability to throw anything away was the one salient trait of my father's that I inherited. Aunt Harriet's letters to me in Yarrow remain among my possessions, tucked in with concert programs, university notes, and other bits and pieces of paper pertaining to the Paristons that I acquired as time went on and I actively began to seek information about them.

All told, there are seventeen or eighteen letters from those summers, to which, in time, I added those she dictated during the year I attended the Vancouver School of Art. Flipping open the envelopes, their messages seem spare and dry, but chewy—like dehydrated fruit.

Phip was in town with Noreen and the babies. I think I frighten them, for whenever I offer to hold one or the other, they end up howling and I sense Noreen fluttering around like a mother crow anxious over its fledglings. I am quite worn out...

Jean and I went to a concert in the park. It was very tinny and quite bad and the air was filled with smoke from people roasting wieners, the calls of children, the rumble of light Sunday traffic rolling along the edge of Borden Park. All a kind of symphony in itself, but I miss you, Curtis.

She wrote this often.

I miss you.

I long for you to be back in town, Curtis. Phillip's words seem awkward and wrong issuing from someone else, when I have become so accustomed to them being borne on your voice. (Jean had written 'born.') *The young man who comes once a week to work in the yard is very willing to take time off from mowing and clipping and pulling weeds, but I believe he must have a problem with adenoids ...*

THE LETTERS I WROTE AUNT HARRIET WERE RAMBLING epistles in which I bemoaned my small-town existence, reviewed ongoing arguments with my mother, and chronicled the comings and goings of people along Main Street, and the few customers who came into the shop.

Sometimes, on his lunch hour, Myron Evington would stop in and shyly go through stacks of magazines. Before I'd finished high school he had completed his crayon-coloured reproductions of flags of the world and had moved on to logos of North American sports teams. As he had once tagged the pages with underwear ads or the nudes from articles reviewing gallery openings in New York or London for me, I now stuck torn pieces of paper in sports magazines for him.

The few times I did manage to get to the library tucked away in the corner of the Municipal Building, I was struck by its shabbiness, the unvarnished shelves, the sun-bleached collection of forgotten novels and out-of-date encyclopedias, the cylindrical coal heater and the awkward stovepipes hooked to it and strung along the ceiling with wires. The Rutherford Library at the university with its cavernous reading room made it difficult for me to remember the feeling of satisfaction and sanctuary this room had once afforded me.

When I did stop in, Myron piled my table with magazines and books he had been saving for months. I had been packing my sketch pad with me whenever I went, and, with each visit, Myron asked me, haltingly, if he might look through it. Even though, by my second trip, he had gone through it page by page, he would always start at the beginning, spending time with the figure drawings I'd made at the university. In particular, the buxom model, Mrs. Hyde-Bennett, fascinated him. A giggle would rest in his throat and he would draw in his breath and hesitantly trace along her abundant breasts with an index finger.

Sometimes, from my upstairs bedroom window, I would spot Myron wandering along the streets late at night, a shuffling, solitary figure whose separateness, whose loneliness was offered to the town with a kind of haunting visibility. If I had been a kinder person, I might have put down what I was reading and joined him. In truth, I was embarrassed to be seen with Myron. I prided myself on having moved past a point of caring what the Yarrow gossips might say about me but there was a corner of my soul that did still care, that wanted to be seen as a presence moving surefootedly along prescribed pathways. The town thought of Myron as 'poor Myron' and, by association, I could see them partnering the two of us as 'a couple of weirdos.'

Like Myron, though, I did escape for solitary rambles through the town and into the countryside. In daylight hours I carried my sketchbook with me so that anyone crossing my path would be certain to see the artist sketching from nature. Even that was a bit weird in Yarrow, but, in my mind, it was a respectable eccentricity. At night, though, I simply tried to remain unseen. Sometimes as I trailed along the railway tracks or the side roads along the edge of town, I felt a kind of hollowness that was almost palpable and alive, pressing from the inside, pressing for escape, release.

There were times when this pressure made it difficult to breathe, brought a pain to my chest. The rage I felt, the self-pity, I would realize much later had to do with the fact that there were spaces within me, spaces surrounding me, for which definition was elusive and troubling. I raged over the absence of romance in my life and I think I felt it not only in the terms of there not being another person to cling to in the night, but the absence of the kind of romantic life I felt Phillip Pariston had experienced at my age.

In a way, I think I coveted the world of Vancouver salons, the cafés and concert halls that sustained him, the weekly routines of music and art lessons, Carnegie lectures and club sports. I had looked often at the few photos of Phillip and his family tucked into the flaps of the maroon portfolio. I envied Phillip his chiselled good looks, his impassioned affair with Harriet. In some ways I think I even coveted his early death. Caught, like Rupert Brooke, frozen in handsomeness, lamented for the broken promises of artistry.

"I can't understand the dark circles under your eyes," my mother commented over supper one day in the August following the completion of my second year at university. She threatened to make an appointment for a checkup with a doctor in St. Paul.

"It's just my reading too late," I mumbled.

"Well, I can't make you turn your light out like I did when you were thirteen." She looked tired herself, I thought. The hours she put in keeping books for the fertilizer plant, coupled with volunteer work at the United Church, were draining—and she was territorial when it came to her kitchen, putting in more hours when she got home.

"No," I said. "And it wouldn't help anyway. I'd just lie awake."

"That comes from the Martindales. My mother's family." She allowed me to pour her a second cup of tea. "None of us could sleep worth a darn."

"Guilty consciences," my father said.

We both looked at him in shock, our mouths open.

My father rarely entered into our conversations and this comment was so out of character we all sat in silence for a minute.

"Just kidding." He looked at me and raised his eyebrows, somehow impishly and sheepishly at the same time.

"I should hope so," my mother sputtered, and then forced a laugh. "Have you heard from the school board?" she asked, grasping for a change of subject. "Mrs. Campbell was in the plant today to pick up Thomas and she said that she heard Mr. Gurney is leaving King George. I think he's been encouraged to retire."

"I didn't apply," I confessed with difficulty over a swallow of tea that seemed to stop where it was along my digestive passageway, waiting for my mother's response.

"What?" Her mouth was agape again, her teacup in midair.

"I've accepted a job teaching junior high in Edmonton."

She set her teacup down with extreme care, as if she feared for its chances of remaining intact.

"My plan is to teach for a couple of years and save my money so I can go to art school in Vancouver."

Without saying anything, she began clearing the supper dishes.

"I'll do that," I said. "You rest."

This was the only time I remember my father reaching over and putting his hand on top of mine. It was a large, heavy hand, callused and rough from his woodworking, but there was an incredible gentleness in his gesture. He shook his head slightly and said, just loudly enough so my mother could hear, "I wouldn't mind if you spent an hour or two at the store tonight sorting through some of those boxes I picked up at Farley's auction yesterday."

WHEN I RETURNED TO THE CITY AT THE END OF THIS second summer, I found a small apartment not far from where Aunt Harriet lived, and, while it meant a long bus ride to and from the school where I'd been posted, I liked being able to walk to her house in fifteen minutes. We fell back into our routine of Sunday visits, often ending with me re-reading a few pages aloud from Phillip's diary.

I discovered early that she was not interested in a sequential reading. She knew the chronology of the passages from other readings over the years. "The first time it was read to me," she recalled, "it was a nurse at St. Mary's. She read it through from beginning to end. Likely she wasn't a nurse for she seemed to have time, more like a nurse's aide, or maybe someone who came in and volunteered. She had a sweet, soothing voice with just the trace of an Irish accent, and she read slowly so it took a long time to get through it.

"In places she would say, 'Oh, I won't read this part—it's too personal' and I would say, 'Please, I need it all.' I did need it all. It was a kind of salve to my soul at the time. Later, Jean would read passages to me, although she's never been a patient reader. It was Jean who noticed there were pages that appeared to have been scissored out or maybe removed with a razor blade. A little mystery there. Phip didn't like to read it aloud although I'm sure he read it on his own."

Once we were settled with our brandy and cocoa, Aunt Harriet would assemble the currents of the evening around her like some kind of invisible comforter, and, wrapped in its folds, she would divine the passage she wanted to hear. She thought of the journal in terms of months.

"January," she might say. "Mid-January, Curtis. Just a bit tonight."

I began to know where the months fell myself, and would find the place she wanted with little difficulty. Years later, when I asked her if I might get the journal copied for myself, she seemed pleased.

"Yes, it will go to Phip of course, but you should have yours too."

It was with this photocopied package in hand that I first read Phillip Pariston's impressions of his days in the sequence in which they had been written. By then I had returned to Edmonton from the Vancouver School of Art and given up the possibility of a penurious career as an artist for my old regularly-paying job with the public school board and Aunt Harriet had begun to give in to the illness that would slowly claim her over the next few months.

More and more often she would nod off as I was reading a passage, and I would find myself pausing and flipping through pages, reviewing silently some of the sequences she found too painful to hear. February, with Phillip's departure to study in Toronto, although it paled in the light of much of what was to come, was a month she avoided. She never said so but I believe she felt it to be a chronicle of lost chances, that if somehow she had been more assertive Phillip would never have left Vancouver, or would have managed to take her along.

February 14, 1917

This evening was my last evening with Hat. It has been miserable. We both have colds and Per came home early from his shift and was quite surly, kept saying how 'honoured' he was to have a Pariston up to his rooms and sorry it was the butler's day off. Finally Hat and I escaped for a walk, but it began to rain and we ducked into a coffee shop on Pender.

Hat kept breaking into tears. Percy McEvoy and Alice Lester came in and sat a couple of booths away and kept looking over at us, making me very nervous. I walked Hat back to her building, but by now it was pouring, a cold rain turning into sleet, and she was soaked and shivering by the time we reached the doorway. I left her with the Valentine card I made yesterday. I'm afraid it only brought on more tears though.

"Don't forget me," she said, when we had our last kiss.

As if that were a possibility.

"OF COURSE," I REMEMBER HER TELLING ME THE ONE TIME she had endured this passage, "I wasn't sure I was pregnant until the end of February."

CHAPTER 7

THE LAST TIME I SAW AUNT HARRIET SHE WAS bedridden but had insisted that Jean make her comfortable in her armchair with an ottoman pulled up so that it became more like a day bed. Her large hands, creased skin and bone, moved restlessly over the afghan that covered her. Her face, too, had divested itself of much of its flesh. She had given up the vanity of wearing glasses, preferring to sit with her eyelids closed. The absence of her glasses, along with the fall of long, white hair, which she had always worn up in my presence, was startling to me.

"You are quiet, Curtis," she observed, her voice as thin as the afternoon light that found its way into the living room through a sparse parting of drapery.

"Just a bit tired." I trolled for time. "We had a staff meeting at work that seemed endless." My new posting was at a junior high in northeast Edmonton where the principal, who had been an army officer during World War II, managed to make the details and delivery of education as painful, I imagined, as the Bastogne assault.

"You should be painting," Aunt Harriet chided me in a hoarse whisper.

"I am," I told her. "In the evenings. It's my sanity—my mental haven. The light is poor, so what I'm doing is fairly tonal. Graphic."

"I'm glad you haven't quit."

Jean hobbled in with tea. She looked as if she were equally a candidate for the armchair and ottoman. With effort, Aunt Harriet lifted one of her hands from the afghan and gestured vaguely.

"You know you're not to smoke," Jean scolded. "Be a darlin'." In an attempt at a wink, she grimaced at me and pointed to a package of cigarettes and a lighter in a small silver tray on the bureau. I put a cigarette to my own mouth and lit it. With my other hand I touched the skeletal fingers which continued to hover, and guided the cigarette to them.

She smoked and sipped a bit of tea as I filled her in on the vicissitudes of teaching art and literature to teenagers, generally sullen and rebellious and obsessed with their own burgeoning sexuality. The ironic aspect of all this, to me, was that I tended to sympathize with their attitudes and preoccupations.

"The 'in' look," I told Aunt Harriet," is for boys to appear like gas-pump jockeys or else rejects from a Beatles audition while the girls are all trying to look like hookers, laden with black eyeliner and teased hair and, if you can believe it, white lipstick. Cleopatra as a vampire."

Aunt Harriet smiled wanly.

Sensing that I had finished my tea and the pastries Jean had left on the coffee table, she had me light another cigarette for her, and, as I again found her fingers, she clasped them around my own for an instant.

"November," she said.

In the case where she kept the diary, the odd bits of salvaged paper, fragments of Phillip Pariston's sketches, curled like haphazard leaves from an autumn storm—a disarray that suggested she'd been shuffling through them—I brushed the loose papers aside, drew the journal out, and opened it with the precision some people acquire in accessing the scriptures, at an entry in the third week in November.

November 23, 1916

The rain has let up and Hat and I walked through slushy streets for what must have been an hour before she had to go to work. I made her come in and dry her stockings and toast her boots in the kitchen, well away from Edwina's baleful eye. Mrs. Cawley made a point of moving the bread she was setting to another counter where she would not have to observe me chafing Hat's chilled feet. The chafing warmed parts of me that brought a blush to my darling's face, and, unable to resist, I wrapped her fully in my arms and kissed her. Edwina, wouldn't you know, chose that moment to come in in her Japanese dressing robe, looking like something out of The Mikado *that has been left out too long and gone bad.*

"I didn't know we were receiving in the kitchen today," she said, and, after glaring at the two of us, swept back out.

Both Hat and I were attempting to stifle giggles, and Mrs. Cawley was making some kind of odd suppressive noise before she let out a whoop of laughter.

I walked Hat back to work and then went to my drawing lesson. Bertram, bless him, is still fighting his cold. In fact, it's worse, and he directed me from a distance. He had praise, though, for my sketches of the skeleton from different angles, although it was difficult at times to know whether he was nodding approval or attempting to clear his sinus passages.

AUNT HARRIET'S HANDS SETTLED BACK TO THE AFGHAN and I thought I heard her laugh softly, but it may have been she was only clearing her throat. I paused in my reading.

"We were so in love," she whispered. "Have you ever been in love, Curtis, truly in love?"

I accepted the question with its soft, barely-discernible words, as rhetorical. But I allowed the pause to widen in circles of thought and memory. Love for me had always been something of a dangerous country where, rather than venturing out, it seemed safer to remain behind locked doors. A couple of false starts when I was going to university in Edmonton. True, there had been that once—in Vancouver—when libido sent me hurtling out into the line of fire. My one-night love affair with Magdalena, a model at the School of Art. The recollection made me snort with derision and I checked quickly to see if the sound had startled Aunt Harriet but she appeared to have fallen, for the moment, asleep. I kept the journal open in case she wanted me to continue, and in the quietness of the room, I found myself remembering, in painful detail, my night with Magdalena.

She was a young Polish émigré who became one of the regular models for our Monday drawing class. She had a kind of pale, northern beauty that brought, I remember, correlations to mind with Harriet Ahlstrom, how she looked—or how I surmised she looked as a young woman—from the few photos and Phillip's sketches among his papers.

When I convinced her to go with me to one of the preview performances at the Queen Elizabeth Playhouse, using the passes regularly given out to art students across the road from the theatre, I remember being giddy with fear and elation. It became almost impossible to focus on the play with Magdalena sitting beside me, as if I'd already divined she would accompany me back to my bachelor apartment where a bottle of sherry sat ready with glasses beside it on my night table and a recording of Van Cliburn's renditions of Chopin lay waiting for the needle to drop. That night my fingers traced the reality of breast and scapula, the fine down along her neck, the trail of vertebrae as Magdalena turned on her side to light a cigarette after we had made love. To the accompaniment of Chopin's lushest nocturnes, she had gently guided me as we worked through the logistics of intercourse, softly moaning, sighing as I peaked, pushing back the wet strands of hair from my forehead as I lay shuddering against her.

When I suggested I might sketch her in chalks, though, she chided me, saying something about a bus driver's holiday, finished a second cigarette, and allowed me to prepay her cab home. It was only later that I realized, with a kind of horrid embarrassment, that the little smile I detected as she kissed me goodnight, was a smile of bemusement, or possibly even worse, pity.

When I invited her to have coffee with me after drawing class the next Monday, I sensed a hesitation before she agreed. It was warm in the coffee shop and she slipped her hooded coat away from her face and shoulders, while still allowing its deep blue wool to frame her blond hair and bare arms. Like Aunt Harriet, she had long, graceful hands that managed to make the lighting and smoking of a cigarette into something of a performance.

I invited her to join me at a Film Society screening later that week at UBC. She set her coffee cup down and took my hand in hers.

"You want to be in love, don't you?" she said.

"What do you mean?"

"You are, I think, being someone else. Acting."

I withdrew my hand.

"I'm just not ..." I felt embarrassment and a kind of anger that I was forced into a position of explanation. "Not very experienced," I said.

"So I am now your experience?" She laughed softly. "How old are you?"

"Twenty-three."

"Ah," she said, drawing the monosyllable in with a drag on her cigarette. "You are so very young and yet very old to be making sex for the first time."

"I don't know." The afternoon was darkening and a light winter drizzle made little, erratic trails of water down the window by our booth. "Maybe it's Canadian. We're probably a bit slower in Canada than in Poland."

"You're funny," she said, finishing her coffee and stubbing out her cigarette. "But I think it is best not to get in ..." she searched for a phrase, "the depth."

"The depth?"

"The deepness. Like a little brother, you are sweet and I am happy to be your beginning experience, but you are, I think, filled with some uncertainness." She put on her coat and drew the hood, tucking her hair back carefully. It made her look older and I realized that she might have done this deliberately to accentuate the fact that she was, indeed, five years my senior.

She squeezed my shoulder as she left.

I sat with a coffee refill, trying to cover the pain of rejection and to show an air of indifference to the world. I turned pages in my art history textbook as if I were actually reading them, and then headed out in the rain to the bus that would take me back to my basement apartment off Cambie Street.

There had been times since Magdalena had charitably eased me away from my virginity, when I felt the stirrings of desire, when I longed to be part of a world where people held hands and listened to romantic songs, arranged weddings, planned for children. But the barrier of my shyness remained solidly present. It was easier to live vicariously in a world of films, books, and plays. And if the brooding, troubled eyes of Marlon Brando made me as dizzy as the shining, haunted gaze of Vivien Leigh, this was a secret I kept to myself. Phillip Pariston smiled across the years at me; Harriet's hand brushed against mine.

Truly in love?

Jean crept in, rearranged the afghan, and poured me another cup of tea. It was tepid but I drank it slowly and brushed crumbs from a piece of her shortbread off the open journal where they left a small, buttery stain.

November 25, 1916

When Harriet finished work I took her home by cab so that she would have time to change for the concert without rushing. For a while I convinced her to sit in her housecoat and we drank some coffee Per had made earlier. She is so beautiful, my Hat, and against the indigo throw on the sofa, and the elusive blues of her wrap, her skin warmed to a golden, almost apricot hue. I did a quick sketch in chalks I had with me, but I failed to capture the colour. Too orange somehow. Hat laughed and said I made her look like a pumpkin. After we made love, I noticed my fingers had left chalk marks on her skin, a touch of blue on her breast, a smudge of crimson along her shoulder blade. Perhaps it is the way to truly interpret the female form.

HE WOULD HAVE WORN A VEST, I THOUGHT. I COULD SEE her unbuttoning it, her large hands working to release the fastenings, slipping suspenders over starched cotton, finding the smaller shirt and collar buttons, releasing the tie, finding the smooth skin of his chest. It would be smooth, a

pale November smoothness, and the large hands trailing
fingertips along his chest as he undid other buttons. The
indigo throw would have been a gift from him, would
have borne them like a sea in their abandonment.

Aunt Harriet stirred and one of her hands moved in
a small tremor as if it were rediscovering that lost afternoon. There would be the reassembling of garments. Hat
getting into her concert clothes. In a photograph of the
Vancouver Women's Musical Society I tracked down in an
archive, they posed in white waists and dark skirts. The
blouses were high-collared and there would have been
a complexity of buttoning. He would help her with the
back of her blouse, her dress boots. His own slim hands
would have been deft with bows, retying his cravat, help-
ing secure the splash of ribbon that kept her hair back and
away from the manoeuvring of the violin.

Jean came in and tapped my shoulder.

"I think I'll just let her sleep awhile," she said. "She
sometimes does. It's so hard for her to move from place to
place now." She walked me to the door. "Thanks for coming, sweetie." She grasped my arm. "She's been asking
about you. Phip will be in town tomorrow for a week or
two. It's about time," she muttered.

IN ADDITION TO A NEW ART PROJECT FOR MY 9D CLASS,
a motley assortment of rejects from the school's options
in music, home ec and shop, I had a grade eight English
class to prepare for, but I took my time, choosing to walk
home across the High Level Bridge rather than take a bus.
The fall colours of the riverbank were muted by the early

dusk except where the odd street light revealed bouquets of poplar gold or the more intense reds of chokecherry and saskatoon bushes.

As I walked, it seemed that I could feel the unforgiving starch of Phillip Pariston's collar against my neck, and I found myself rubbing my fingers against my jacket lapels, as if ridding myself of the residue of chalk. For an instant I felt I could even smell the salt of sea air. Was I insane? I stopped and grasped a cold railing of the bridge, looked out to the winding expanse of the North Saskatchewan River, and breathed in the crisp inland air from a breeze that had begun to build, a breeze that plucked laughter from my lips and sent it scattering into the autumn night.

THE DAY AUNT HARRIET DIED, I'D SPENT THE NOON HOUR meeting with my art club, a few students who came in once a week for additional drawing lessons, and to make posters for school functions or design graphics for the yearbook. This day in late November, I'd challenged them to create a pencil sketch, focusing entirely on negative space, of an antique three-tiered plate stand I'd borrowed from a heap of items donated for a PTA rummage sale. I'd put the club through the paces of many of the design exercises I'd worked through in my art options at the U of A or during my year at the Vancouver School of Art. We'd already completed a series of contour drawings and gesture drawings, and some exercises in negative space were next in a sequence in one of the sketchbooks I'd kept.

These eight or nine students were good, most of them mature beyond their junior high years, although a couple of the grade eight girls were given to small fits of giggling, particularly if they caught the attention of Wolfgang, a grade nine boy who looked a bit like Ricky Nelson.

I placed the plate stand on a table, letting it stand in relief against a wooden screen draped with rumpled canvas.

"The space surrounding an object can, in many ways, be as crucial, as telling as what we might consider the obvious focus of a picture. I want you to explore with your drawing pencils the space around the plate stand, shade it, using cross-hatching or layered shading if you want to. Try to get a sense of the texture and wrinkles of the backdrop. Think of the space behind the object, between the verticals of the spooled legs, around and within the handle, the circular edges as the actual picture." I demonstrated by sketching in one corner of a piece of poster paper I'd tacked up.

"We call this negative space," I told them, "and you might think of it as a kind of 'nothing' area, but your compositions will be stronger if you think of it as ... well, having a life of its own."

As they ate their sandwiches and worked on their drawings, I was called over the PA system down to the school office.

Jean was on the phone. "She's gone, Curtis." There was hardly any volume to her voice. "She just slipped away, the poor dear."

I could sense her struggling to keep from crying, and I discovered I could barely speak myself. Finally I managed to tell her I'd be over as soon as classes dismissed for the afternoon.

Back in the art room I busied myself finishing the demonstration piece. The negative spaces grew in definition, became continental masses, each a dark geography— unique, suggestive, associative, a kind of small homage to the spaces Aunt Harriet must have been encountering in all of the years of her blindness. The spaces I kept finding in her life story.

CHAPTER 8

I WAS SURPRISED MY PARENTS CAME TO AUNT Harriet's funeral.

"I thought you didn't care for her," I said to my mother as she pinned into place a liver-coloured felt hat.

"How can you say such a thing?" She smiled at me and, catching sight of lipstick trespassing on her teeth, blotted it with one of the tissues from a box on my hallstand. "It's true we were never close, but it was mainly distance that separated us. If Hartley could selflessly devote himself to such a—" She began checking her handbag as if the right word were somehow temporarily misplaced with house keys and pill bottles. "Such an incapable person, I'm sure I've always stood behind him."

"If you don't get a move on, we'll be late." My father waited in limbo, halfway in and halfway out of the apartment door.

"It doesn't start for an hour," I said, slipping into the black trench coat that I'd recently purchased but couldn't afford. I had rationalized that it would last close to a lifetime. Aunt Harriet would have approved, I felt, its gabardine smoothness.

"I don't want to park a mile away." My father glowered at my mother who had decided she didn't like the angle of her hat and was repinning it.

We were the first to arrive at the chapel, except for Phip who was busy sorting things out with an organist, a bilious young man who eventually hunched into position and began pumping out music, themes I recognized from recordings Aunt Harriet had in her collection.

Spotting us, Phip came over. He had thickened in the years since he brought his first wife, the bounteous June, to meet us, but I recognized the long, slender hands of his mother now, and something in the set of his face, perhaps the high cheekbones that Aunt Harriet also had.

My mother managed one of her few hugs and apologized for Bradley being unable to take time from work to come to the funeral.

I hugged him too.

"Thanks," Phip said to me, "for being with her so much over these past few years."

My mother looked at me oddly.

"You didn't tell me you spent a lot of time with Harriet," she said after we'd found a place to sit that afforded a good view of the casket and a reasonable vantage for watching those who entered the sanctuary. I wondered if the white roses that engulfed the casket had been chosen deliberately by Phip for their lack of colour, a reminder of a life lived largely without the sensibilities of colour and linear form. I would have chosen red, the red of the claret Aunt Harriet enjoyed with our dinners, a red that I felt infused the darkness that had enveloped her over the past forty years.

"You have secrets," my mother noted with an aggrieved air.

"No," I said. "But I've been away from home for seven years. I didn't think you'd want to know everything I was doing."

She sighed and patted my hand. "I don't mind. You can have as many secrets as you want. I don't expect that you should tell me everything. Oh, look." The liver hat swivelled. "There's what's-her-name. My god, she looks awful."

Jean seemed to have shrunk in size, if that were possible. With Phip now at her side, they looked like a giant and a dwarf, a circus couple. He escorted her to an empty pew at the front.

"You'd think that Noreen and the children might have come." My mother noted the absence of Phip's wife and his two daughters. My father grunted.

An usher came over with late-arriving programs. On the cover was the sketch of a young woman's face, and I recognized a detail from the chalk drawing Phillip Pariston had made of Phip's mother, the nude on the living-room wall. Out of the corner of my eye, I watched my mother's face for some sign of outrage but she failed to associate the face with the sketch that had so irked her on that visit when Bradley and I were children.

"You'd think they'd have put a photo of Harriet on the cover," she whispered loudly to my father and me. "Maybe it's a Toronto thing."

The melancholy young man at the organ allowed a chord (something by Bach, I thought) to swell and sink before moving into an air that was more familiar to me. Obviously not something written for the organ but something transposed.

"What an odd-sounding thing," my mother poked me. "That's a hymn I've never heard before. Do you have any idea what it is?"

"It's an air," I said, "that Harriet once played at the Vancouver Women's Musical Society."

I HAD SUPPER WITH PHIP A FEW DAYS LATER. HE WAS catching a plane back to Toronto the next morning.

"On me," he said, waving his hand like a benediction over the menu. We were at the MacDonald Hotel, chosen, I suspected, because of the times he had eaten there as a younger man with his mother and Uncle Hartley. "You've been very caring and I want you to know how much I appreciate that." His words were a bit flannel-edged, but I thought he had earned the right to get drunk this evening if he felt like it. The waiter finished a bottle of wine with the filling of our glasses and Phip nodded when he asked about a replacement.

"To Aunt Harriet." I raised my glass, "She was very caring to me too—at a time when I needed it."

"Mother." Phip accepted my toast.

He told me about his week as we worked our way through the steak specials. The house had been sorted through with the help of a tearful Jean; a real estate agent had been acquired; and Jean herself had been settled into a senior's complex. Over baked Alaska, he brought me up to date on Noreen, who was teaching again, while his daughters attended a private school in the city.

"They weren't that close to Mom. I guess if we'd visited more ... But Noreen's so attached to her own mother. And Mom absolutely refused to move again, come back to Toronto after Hartley died." He signalled the waiter to refill our glasses.

"She left you a few things." He snapped open a brief-case that had been parked by his chair throughout our meal. "Jean gathered them together into this envelope."

I recognized Jean's cribbed writing in the words scrawled on the outside of the envelope. "For Curtis."

"A letter and a few photographs. I think she hoped I'd have been more interested in them myself. Yeah ..." His face became flushed with the wine, and fatigue had settled into lines I hadn't noticed before, around his eyes and mouth. "I used to look through this stuff. But I couldn't live it the way she did. Day in and day out." He pushed the package toward me. "I had copies made of the photos."

"She never had any photos of your grandfather Ahlstrom, did she?" I caught myself tracing my fingers around the edge of the manila envelope. "I wonder if you have his features."

"Could be. Nobody's ever seen a picture of him. I've had people ask me if I was Danish or German. I guess ..."

He stopped in mid-sentence to light a cigarette. "I guess I don't really care. I got really tired of living in the past. I think Dad—Hartley—did too, but he was such a patient man. I think it was especially hard for him." He paused, surveyed the room, caught the waiter's eye, and ordered brandies.

"Hard for him?" I made an effort to make my hands settle on the envelope, unopened on the table. I couldn't decide whether I should open it in Phip's presence or not.

"Well, you know, hard that he was never really the love of her life."

"He knew that?"

Phip snorted and lit another cigarette. He held a smoke the way she did, the cigarette seeming to become an extension of his long fingers.

"He knew. Thank god he was willing to settle for what she was willing to give, I guess. Affection certainly. She was fond of him—and grateful. You can go a long way on gratitude."

The brandies arrived in warmed snifters and, when I inhaled, the fumes caught and burned inside, making me gasp, bringing tears to my eyes. Phip laughed and, reaching over, slapped me playfully on the back.

"I can see why she liked you," he said.

"Really?" I sputtered.

"You have kind of another-world air about you. I don't mean that unkindly. You look to me like someone who's right at home listening to long-hair music at the Jubilee on Sunday afternoon. I never was, you know. Sooner go to the ball game with Hartley." He rummaged in the briefcase and brought out another manila envelope. "Thought you might want to have these too. Bits and pieces of the sketches she kept, you know, like holy relics. I guess you know the stories behind these."

"Are you sure...?" My hand caressed the envelope.

"I kept a couple of the more complete ones, but you can have the rest.

"You kept the diary, didn't you?"

"Yeah. She wanted that in the family."

"She let me have it copied."

"Good. Maybe you can do something with it. Historical interest and all that." He was searching in his briefcase again. "Ah, the final part of her bequest to you. Now, this I wouldn't mind owning. I wonder if she had any idea what these little sketches are going for these days. However, she's very definite in her will, the Tom Thomson for Curtis."

He placed a cardboard handkerchief box on top of the two manila envelopes, slipped off the cover, and drew back the tissue paper from around the small painting.

"Another brandy?"

I could see Phip was settled in for the evening. Shaking my head, I made my excuses. I was developing a small handbook on perspective for my grade eight art option and I had to have it ready to duplicate the following morning. I squeezed his shoulder as I got up. "I'm going to miss her," I said. He raised his brandy glass and nodded by way of farewell.

When I got back to my apartment, I put on a pot of coffee and forced myself to work woozily through the perspective examples on spirit duplicator masters, even making myself redo one of the two-point diagrams when a slip of the ruler created a line that slithered off at a drunken angle. It was midnight by the time I was finished, but the coffee had done its work and I was wide awake, if exhausted.

I opened the envelope Jean had labelled. It contained six photographs that Phip had copied. The studio portrait of Phillip that Aunt Harriet had asked Jean to show me on two or three occasions. Another studio photo showing the four Pariston men, Alfred—"Old Grand"—seated on an elaborately carved chair, Alfed Jr. behind him flanked by Phillip and Everett. Only Everett in his army uniform managing anything approaching a smile. There were three snapshots of Harriet herself. It was odd that I'd never seen these in my many visits. They must, to begin with, have been among the papers secured in the pockets of the diary cover. There were no markings of the oily rain on them, no scorch marks, or evidence of having been damaged by water or snow.

Perhaps they had only been rediscovered when Jean cleaned through things as she and Phillip got the house ready for sale. Two appeared to have been taken on the same occasion, probably an outing to Stanley Park, Harriet wearing a jaunty tam, grinning, leaning against the gigantic trunk of a Douglas fir, in the other balanced on a piece of the seawall, hugging herself against the wind. The third was a head shot with a couple of small roses tucked into her hair, and a dark ribbon around her neck. The smile was faint here; the eyes a revelation. It could only have been Phillip behind, I guessed, a hand-held Kodak. I can see him positioning Harriet to give her carefully curled hair a soft sheen. Even if his eyes were, for a few seconds, behind the camera lens, her eyes were rich with the knowledge of a lover's gaze.

The sixth photograph was a rather posed 'candid' of Phillip at work in the studio Alfred Jr. had let him set up in a corner of the gatehouse. The snapshot showed him sketching at a drawing table in the midst of shelves holding plaster casts, baskets and pots stuffed with rolled papers, brushes, pens and pencils. I had seen this one before but not for about three years. I placed the six along the top of a bookshelf I had assembled out of bricks and boards.

Along with the photographs, there was one page of a letter, an elaborate scrawl in lavender-coloured ink:

It was a surprise, Harriet, to hear from you after all this time. Everett's death has been, as you say, a blow to all of us. I think Alfred shall never recover. In some ways I am grateful that Father left us a few months before. You know how he doted on his grandsons. I have barely been able to get through each day myself. It is only to be strong for Alfred that I resist giving in to utter despair. The house is so silent and I cannot make myself even think of music, although Mrs. Brampton Carlisle says she will send her driver and have me brought by force, if necessary, to her soiree next Wednesday to hear the Remelli brothers if I don't promise to come on my own. Alfred says for me to go, that I cannot become a total recluse, and so I may, but with greatly mixed feelings.

The news that you have healed well is, of course, good. I am reluctant, though, to place any requests for support before Alfred these days, and, in truth, the money we sent you following Phillip's passing was, I feel, more than generous. However, for Phillip's sake, I do enclose a money order

THE SECOND PAGE OF THE LETTER WAS MISSING AND I could imagine it being clutched in Aunt Harriet's hands, crumpled or torn, before she decided that Edwina's perfidy might need to be kept as a record of how the Paristons had chosen to treat her and Phip.

Everett, I remembered her saying, had, on a warm day in April after the war ended, hobbled the few blocks down to English Bay from the Pariston House and, witnessed by a scattering of people out to enjoy the early morning sun from the beach or the walk along it, calmly removed his clothing and walked into the sea. A few watched but no one raced into the chilly water to try and rescue him when he had gone far enough beyond his depth to commit suicide. He simply disappeared, walking along the ocean floor. He hadn't gone out all that far, though, and his body was retrieved within hours.

"Mrs. McTavish, who'd been my landlady, wrote me about Everett." Aunt Harriet was patient with my bouts of questioning. "Her sister had settled in Vancouver during the war, and she knew of our interest in the family. When I found out, of course, I wrote, but I suspect the letter never got to Alfred. It is one of several things for which I have never forgiven Edwina." At that point Harriet hit out with her hand in what appeared to be an involuntary motion, knocking over a vase on the coffee table, and what she said next startled me.

"That bitch." Her fingers searched for the overturned vase and righted it. "That selfish bitch."

EDWINA, AUNT HARRIET ADMITTED, HAD BEEN SOMETHING of a beauty back when the widower Alfred Pariston Jr. met her during a business trip to London.

"Somehow she managed to enchant Phillip's father, and with the Pariston wealth in the balance, she didn't have any second thoughts about giving up her music hall career. I heard her sing once when she'd had too much to drink at a Pariston gathering and, believe me, she was wise to have retired from the stage when she did.

"Christmas, of course, was their anniversary," she told me that first December that we had grown into the comfortable routine of spending Sundays together once or twice a month. "Trust Edwina to try and upstage Jesus. She was most unhappy that Phillip had insisted upon inviting me for Christmas dinner."

I had been reading her a passage from Phillip's journal.

Edwina is behaving like Scrooge before his reformation, he had written. *She actually told Dads to ask me not to invite Harriet. I said that would be fine but then not to expect me either as I would be spending the day with Hat. Dads sputtered around a bit and then said no, that would never do. Everett would be home and he wanted both of his sons there. He was sure Edwina could be persuaded to include Harriet. Poor Dads. It seems he is always caught in the middle of things.*

Officially I am giving Hat a necklace of opals. For her eyes only, I have scrolled the nude sketch I committed to paper last weekend and bound it with a piece of red ribbon.

"LATER, WHEN WE WERE TOGETHER AFTER ALL THOSE terrible months of missing one another, I returned it to him for safekeeping. I remember him protecting its chalked surface with a page of onionskin paper as he slid it into the papers he kept inside the bindings of his journal."

"The opals?"

"I don't know whatever happened to them," Aunt Harriet sighed. "Lost," she added but I noticed the tips of her fingers moving against one another as if she could feel the smooth surface of the jewels, remembering their sequence in the necklace as one might the beads of a rosary.

CHAPTER 9

FOLLOWING AUNT HARRIET'S DEATH, I DECIDED to continue attending Edmonton's symphony concerts. I had, as she predicted, acquired a taste for classical music, but the Sunday afternoon trips to the Jubilee Auditorium were, as well, a kind of homage to the years we had attended together.

It was during intermission at one of these on a dreary February Sunday that I ran into Walter Mandriuk again. When he'd begun teaching, he'd taken a post out of town, not far from the farm where he'd grown up. We'd talked on the phone a few times and even exchanged Christmas cards for a couple of years. He'd tried to arrange a get-together when he was in the city for his district's teachers' convention but I'd been unable to find a time to meet him and, after that, we'd lost touch. Now he was waving at me from across the foyer, hurrying through the crowd to the corner where I stood, nursing a glass of sherry.

"Curtis. Hey, Curt!" For a moment I thought he was going to give me a hug, but he settled for shaking my hand and squeezing my arm. "This is incredible."

"Do you come to these often?" I asked him. "I've never seen you here before."

"Just this past year." He ducked his head, shaking the still-bleached hair into place. "A friend of mine was ushering for the evening performance and I started coming with him. He's moved to Calgary now, but I sort of got into the habit. Thought I'd change my tickets for afternoons, though."

As we compared notes, it turned out he had moved into the city and was teaching phys. ed. in the junior high not far from my own school. We agreed to meet after the performance and go for an early supper, choosing one of the restaurants we'd gone to the odd time we'd grabbed a supper together when we were taking classes. It had gone through a series of transitions and was, in its latest guise, a gasthaus with its walls given over to a collection of cuckoo clocks that created a monumental din of wheezing and cuckooing with the striking of the hour. A waiter in lederhosen with red knees and a red nose served us wiener schnitzel and potato dumplings, at times breaking into a wispy yodel, a kind of unconscious vocal accompaniment to German folk music fighting to be heard through the crackling and hissing of a dying sound system.

As the supper progressed, Walter and I became weak with laughter and left, foregoing the apple strudel, knowing that it would bring us to the apex of another hour and a renewed din of mechanical bird calls.

"I'm out of strudel," I told Walter, "but come over for a drink at my apartment." Walter owned a car and had offered to begin picking me up in the mornings and driving me to work. The drink seemed like the smallest of prepayments for the favour.

Over supper, I had filled him in on the time I'd spent in Vancouver at art school, and I updated him on my ongoing relationship with Aunt Harriet over the years. He seemed drawn to the Tom Thomson, which I had hanging over the sofa with a couple of framed calendar prints of paintings by the Group of Seven. As I poured brandies and put on a pot of coffee, I told him what I knew of the painting and its acquisition by Aunt Harriet.

"I remember you going over to see your old aunt," Walter said. "Quite a story."

"That's her in the snapshots on top of the bookcase."

"A looker," Walter observed. "And who's this dude?" He had picked up the studio photo of Phillip Pariston. I sketched in more of the story.

"Criminal to be that handsome," Walter laughed. "He must have had everyone swooning over him."

Walter did hug me at the door as he left. "Curt-boy," he said, "I can't tell you how good it is to catch up with you again. Tell you the truth, I was feeling pretty down with Josh gone to Calgary. It's funny how things go around, isn't it?" He smelled of Old Spice and wool and brandy.

"Funny," I agreed.

"See you in the morning."

I put on a Brahms piano concerto and allowed its crystalline notes to add their own kind of refraction to the events of the afternoon and early evening. The coffee maker's gurgling claimed my attention and, getting a cup, I picked up Phillip Pariston's photograph from the bookshelf and curled into the armchair. The more the photos sat out, the less I had taken note of them over the weeks and Walter's comment about Phillip's handsomeness made me look at it again with new eyes. Of course some of the handsomeness was achieved through the photographer's art. Lighting brought a glow to his skin and found highlights in his hair that were less noticeable in the snapshot of him in his workroom. But there was no doubt about it really. Phillip Pariston had the kind of good looks that would have turned heads, a presence with the angular features and limpid eyes that Hollywood photographers had discovered in the beautiful young men of the 1920s and 1930s—Ramon Novarro, Gary Cooper, Robert Taylor.

"I wish you could have met him," Aunt Harriet said more than once. "He was like no one else I have ever seen. People just wanted to do things for him the minute they saw him. He had his grandfather and Alfred Jr. wrapped around his finger, and the servants, they'd do anything to please him. But, of course, he never really asked much of anyone."

February can be alleviated with such things as strong coffee, piano music by Brahms, soft lamplight. Putting the photograph aside, I got out my copy of Phillip's journal, its cardboard covers shellacked and lined inside with marbled papers retrieved from a demonstration for an art class at school. It was possible for me to open it to a late January entry without flipping pages.

January 29, 1917

Spent the evening with Hat. Per was on the late shift so no fear of his coming upon us. We built up the fire in the fireplace and made ourselves as naked as savages. I'd forgotten my chalks or I would have done another sketch of Hat with her hair down. She has put on some weight and it is very becoming to her, although she was not pleased when I brought this to her attention. I assured her the weight had distributed itself to great effect but this only prompted the propulsion of a pillow at me. In a minute, though, she brought another pillow and the star-patterned quilt she has finished sewing to join me on the floor. Bolstered thus, we made love so slowly and gently at first, building and building to that sweet explosion that came in waves, leaving us spent but impossibly happy.

Old Grand was still up when I came in. I could see the light on in his study and I went in to say goodnight. He was reading Vanity Fair, *a treat he allows himself when he has trouble sleeping. He looked at me with question marks in his shaggy eyebrows, wondering, I suspect, if I am fully ready to throw myself into my studies in Toronto. We chatted about nothing consequential, though, and I nearly fell asleep in the wingback chair. Now I am somewhat awake again but, I think, not for long. Not so long as to finish a chapter in* Henry Esmond, *which Old Grand has loaned me.*

I close my eyes and see you, Hat, and kiss you and kiss you …

I REMEMBER THAT YEAR, WHEN I MANAGED TO TAKE A winter term at the Vancouver School of Art, I spent August finding rooms and getting settled in. In my rambles through the West End, I found myself stopping often in front of the old Pariston mansion and one Saturday I had lunch in the restaurant that had appropriated the south parlour, the drawing room and the first-floor library. I tried to imagine how it would have looked filled with Edwina's furniture and knick-knacks, the Persian rugs and draperies she prized for the way in which they modulated the sound of music during her soirees as much as for their intricate designs. Aunt Harriet had given me the details; they remained vividly in her mind.

"It made me think of something out of the Arabian Nights," I recalled her telling me. "Wood polished to a high gleam. Large oriental vases. A conservatory filled with tropical plants. I would go from there to the two-room flat that Papa and I shared on Cordova Street and I would feel like I was two different people—one who went about on Phillip's arm, the other—what? A shopgirl. Someone who scrubbed her own floors. Someone who mended her father's shirts, darned stockings, and put cardboard inside her shoes when the soles wore thin.

"We lived in two or three rooming houses," Aunt Harriet told me, "and then Per met Mrs. Mezzkis at a party and, when one of her upstairs tenants moved out, we got their flat and it was nicer than anything we'd been in before in Vancouver. Mrs. Mezzkis had quite a crush on Per. He was a good-looking man, very tall with a mop of whitish-blond hair that some Scandinavian men have. She would trot up the stairs with bowls of soup and plates of pastry, always breathless by the time she reached our door."

The music teacher at the secondary school she'd been attending had urged Per to have Harriet take music lessons, I remembered Aunt Harriet telling me. "Mrs. Wilson arranged for a friend of hers to begin teaching me violin. I loved going over to Mr. Stelmecky's place. Maybe it was because his wife always had a snack waiting for me. They had a house just off Denman, not far from English Bay. The funny thing was that, depending on what route I took, I sometimes ended up walking by the Pariston mansion in the West End.

"The house stood way back from a wrought iron fence. It was something to see with its gables and turrets and a great verandah that extended into a carriage port. Its walls were kind of a dark stone—Phillip told me later that it had all been quarried on Gabriola Island—which gave it a rather solemn, forbidding look, although ivy had taken hold on some of the walls and the verandah had white pillars.

"To my thirteen-year-old eyes, "Aunt Harriet had recalled, "it looked incredibly grand and I'd walk slowly along the block it covered, running my fingers along the curlicues of wrought iron as I went. Once in a while, I'd notice boys playing in the yard, calling to one another, tossing a rugby ball or heading with their racquets to the courts in back of the building." She remembered that these could be seen by walking along the avenue just north of the house.

"It's odd, isn't it," she mused during one of those long evenings of brandy and music, "to think of how lives are— what?—destined to connect? They exist in their separate tracks and you realize afterwards, yes, I wandered by the home of the boy who would grow up and become my lover, and the sound of me running a stick along the fence spilled into his shouts to his brother, the very air we were breathing, currents crossing, mingling."

When I had eaten all I could of a carrot and kelp salad, I asked the woman at the till if I might see some of the upstairs rooms.

"It's just storage," she said. "And the Trust keeps them locked except for our own storage unit."

A poster shop had assembled itself in what had been the conservatory. It contained no plants at all now, and the glass panes were blocked with paper rectangles from which peered the visages of Marlene Dietrich, W.C. Fields, and the Beatles.

I asked the proprietor if she remembered the house from an earlier time.

"Oh yes, dear," she exclaimed. "It was a dance hall during the war. I remember kicking up my heels on those hardwood floors. Seems to me people could rent it too, you know, for weddings, receptions. That kind of thing."

Huge trees had grown up in the yard so that it was difficult to see the windows on the second and third floors. I strolled across the street to gain the perspective that Aunt Harriet had as a teenager off to her violin lessons.

"One summer day," she told me when a conversation had pooled around her years in Vancouver, "I think it must have been a year or two after I'd been going to the Stelmecky's for lessons, I was walking by the mansion and the whole front lawn was given over to a party. There was a band playing and ladies in summer dresses that seemed almost to have been fashioned from the petals of flowers. They wore huge hats covered with feathers and bows, and the men were all in fine suits. I think I must have stood there gaping for ten minutes and then one of the waiters with a tray of glasses came close by the fence and winked at me and I hurried on, knowing I was going to be late for my lesson. I remember feeling that I'd caught a glimpse of some rare, exotic world, a world that existed quite apart from the waterfront."

I couldn't help wondering if Edwina hadn't blocked Harriet's coming to live with them after Phip had been born, what would have happened to the house if Harriet and her son had become the inheritors. In the quirks of circumstance, though, I would never have found myself in a position where I would have had a second thought about the building. If she had been taken in by the Paristons, she would never have met my Uncle Hartley and the connection would have failed to exist.

Although the crush of building in Vancouver's West End, even in the 1960s, made it difficult to find a vantage where it would be possible to view the house as people once did, from the edge of its spacious grounds, it still dominated the area. Only later, when the West End became a welter of high-rises, did it seem to shrink. Declared a heritage building, it was allowed to remain, its stone exterior darkening from year to year until it became close to black in the 1980s when a fire raged through it and it was finally demolished.

CHAPTER 10

"**S**HE HAD EXTRAVAGANT TASTES," MY MOTHER said, carefully replacing the snapshots on the bookcase. "That's the first thing I remember about her when Hartley married her. I expect it came from her hobnobbing with those Vancouver swells."

My mother had come in for one of her days with specialists and, after being prodded, probed, scanned, and x-rayed, she had decided to stay the night with me and catch the bus home tomorrow.

"I guess the wedding was a real splash. Of course Hartley was proud that she had pearls and white orchids and a tiara in her hair that looked like it was set with diamonds. And Phip had a black velvet suit. Can you imagine the expense?"

She removed her oxfords and surveyed the living room from the armchair. "You've got some of her pictures. I remember that little oil painting."

"It's a Thomson."

"Hartley never paid any attention to how a room was decorated. I think it amused him that she would seem to know in her mind's eye where things were. Bradley and Bonita have been doing jigsaw puzzles and then framing them. They've finished *Blue Boy* and *Pinky*, and they're working on *The Last Supper*."

My brother had married his high-school steady, the daughter of the druggist in Yarrow. I told my mother I was glad that they had discovered the connubial bliss to be found in a mutual passion for jigsaw puzzles.

"Don't be snide," she said.

"No, really—I think it's great."

"Of course it was in the 1920s and people like Hartley had some money although nothing like it was made out to be. We wouldn't have known a stock or a bond if it'd jumped up and slapped us in the face!" My mother was skillful at juggling topics. "But when I think of the expense involved in that wedding when she couldn't see any of it for herself. I heard that somehow or other they even managed to get champagne for the wedding supper. I kept thinking of how your grandmother had ruined her eyes sewing for people, and here was Hartley serving champagne."

The day had been exhausting for her and she decided to make an early night of it, turning in in my room after I'd gotten blankets out to make myself a bed on the sofa. I was restless, though. I drank coffee and watched an old Gary Cooper movie on television, an odd picture with Cooper in elegant clothes playing an artist who moved easily among what my mother would have called a bunch of British swells. Aunt Harriet told me that Phillip Pariston had been tall and lanky. Of course she had never had the chance to see what Gary Cooper looked like. I asked her once if anyone in the films of the time reminded her of Phillip. She recalled thinking that Richard Barthelmess had a kind of natural gracefulness that made her think of Phillip, but they really didn't look alike.

"We didn't go to the movies much. Just the odd one. Our evenings were busy. I had violin lessons two nights a week and I was a spare in two or three orchestras. Phillip actually had more time although he would fill in on the piano if somebody needed him. When we could we took in some of the tea dances in the Hotel Vancouver. Theatre and concerts.

"I wore the opals Phillip had given me for Christmas when we went to see Nijinsky in the Ballets Russes. We went with Alfred Jr. and Edwina, and I think Edwina was more focused on my necklace than on Cleopatra."

"Nijinsky in Vancouver?"

"It was something to watch Edwina in the Pariston's box at the Opera House. You might have thought Edwina herself was ready to take centre stage. I remember she had a headdress that sported a bunch of egret feathers. She never sat still; she was forever arching around to see who was in neighbouring boxes and peering over the railing to see who she might spot below, fluttering her fan—more egret feathers. It seemed to me there was this kind of perpetual blur of rather bedraggled feathers. She wore a gown with a lot of elaborate beading and I think she knew that, by moving even the slightest bit, the glass beads would catch the light of the chandelier and she would literally sparkle.

"I lost all thought of Edwina, though, when the curtain opened and there we were in the glow of the desert sun with great Egyptian columns in relief against the sky. Oh, it was something, Curtis. And then there was Nijinsky, a dark slave, and Cleopatra so mysteriously beautiful, her half-naked figure emerging as long bands of silk were unwound. I know I gasped and I think half of the audience did as well. Her skin glowed—if you can believe it—a kind of translucent sea green."

I remember Aunt Harriet laughing softly. "Rather amazing. Vancouverites loved their music. Opera. Ballet. You see, I knew there would be work for a violinist and I studied hard. Papa didn't begrudge the lessons, and by then I was working in The Bay in their music department during the day so I could pay for lessons in the evening."

I browsed through January in my copy of Phillip's diary, but there was no entry for the day the family attended the Ballets Russes. In fact there were few entries in January. A Carnegie lecture on George Cruikshank with Old Grand. Chinese New Year when Harriet and Phillip had gone down to Chinatown to watch the celebration. The Vancouver Women's Musical Society at the Hotel Vancouver (Harriet having to ask for time off to fill in with the strings). Waiting for news of the Somme. Wondering if Everett had been in the action. Another trip to the Opera House to see *The Miracle Man*—but without Harriet. The diary entries became cryptic as Phillip's departure for Toronto grew closer.

During a taping session, she told me, "I'll always remember the day he left. I was able to get time off work and Phillip had been adamant that no one from the family was to come to the train station, that he wanted to say all of his farewells at home. I'd even been included in the supper Edwina had organized the previous evening. But the day he left there were just the two of us, and after he'd checked his luggage, we ordered pots of tea at the station café. There seemed to be steam in the air, not just from our tea, and it made Phillip's face shiny. Isn't it odd? I remember sitting, holding hands under the tabletop, the pressure of his fingers against my own, his face softly shining like the face of some incredible angel. I can't remember a thing we said, just that wonderful face and the feeling of emptiness when he was gone.

"I think we wrote to each other every day to start with."

February 18, 1917

I am in Toronto at last and, I must admit, there is a feeling of electricity. Radcliffe Malthus was kind enough to meet my train. He is a flamboyant character, but endearing, and I think he has organized the next couple of weeks so that there will be few spare moments. Perhaps this is a good thing these first days away from Hat.

Tomorrow I am to take my portfolio to a friend of Radcliffe's who is taking students for drawing and painting instruction. Apparently he studied at L'École des Beaux Arts in Paris and is involved here, in Toronto, with the Arts and Letters Club as

Radcliffe is himself. Later we are to have lunch at the club and Radcliffe will introduce me around. I think he is determined I shall get to know every artist in the city within the next month. He has a story to tell about each one and I believe he told many of them as we travelled around town in his touring car.

It was a relief to finally get to Malthus House, which is very elegant. I have a large bedroom and sitting room, which Radcliffe says I am to convert into a studio as I see fit. He has begun the process himself by installing a drawing desk, his gift of welcome for me, an oak desk with an adjustable tilt top. Much finer than my old makeshift one at the gatehouse.

Once details have been sorted out, it seems Radcliffe will be heading to the States to spend some time in the south, New Orleans in particular. He is anxious to explore the French Quarter with his camera. He is apologizing already for leaving me alone at Malthus House so soon after my arrival. I assured him I will be most comfortable and do not mind, at all, having time to myself. It is in my mind to get into a strict regimen of practice.

I am weary after the long trip, and the lengthy supper with my host, but I feel I shall not sleep for a while yet, time I shall use to begin a letter to Hat.

"IT WAS IN EARLY MARCH I WROTE AND TOLD HIM THAT I was pregnant." I remember Aunt Harriet getting out of her chair and moving restlessly around the room, knocking over a table lamp, which she quickly righted. "In a way, I think I was ecstatically happy. Phillip would have to return and marry me. There was never a doubt in my mind."

She heard the question mark in my silence.

"Things are never so simple," Aunt Harriet said. "My letter was not received before he decided to return to Vancouver for a visit. Old Grand had had a minor stroke, I think. The family had telephoned Phillip to see if he might come back for at least a few days. So you can imagine him on a train headed west, my letter on a train headed east. In the meantime I lost my balance on Mrs. Mezzki's stairway, fell down half a flight, and lost the baby."

Aunt Harriet wept when she told me this and then brushed angrily at her tears. "It seems so silly ... so small ... to cry about this with everything that was happening in the world. With what Everett was going through in Europe. My God.

"I was hemorrhaging badly and when Per realized what was happening to me, he went crazy. "He blew up at Mrs. Mezzkis who was dancing around hollering in Lithuanian about the blood on her hall carpet, and took a strip off the head nurse at St. Paul's. I think he was thrown out of the hospital and barred from returning. Later he got into a fight at work and would have been jailed if he hadn't been able to convince a police captain that he was needed to nurse me in my illness and distraction."

Aunt Harriet found her chair again. Exhaustion seemed to have followed close on her tears. "I was distracted," she whispered. "I wanted Phillip so desperately. When Per decided we should pack up our belongings—heaven knows we didn't have much—and head for Montreal, I saw it as a small shaft of light in the darkness. Montreal was so much closer to Toronto than

Vancouver. I really wasn't well enough to travel but, for Per, I put on a bold face.

"Phillip had given me a copy of *Tess of the D'Urbervilles* and, when I wasn't sleeping, I think I read the entire way. Can you imagine reading *Tess of the D'Urbervilles* all across Canada in my condition? It's no wonder I was ready to be hospitalized by the time I reached Montreal."

I remember, at this point in her chronicle, she did seem to give in to exhaustion and slept briefly as I sat by her. The Hardy novel, I realized, offered an ironic counterpoint that had not been lost on Harriet Ahlstrom as she thought back over this journey. Tess's seducer, of course, had been very different from Phillip Pariston, but there was the social distance, and I remembered that in the Hardy novel a letter gone astray—had it been slipped under a door only to be lost under the edge of a rug on the other side? Changing the course of events in Tess's young life?

In 1917, the mail travelled across Canada by train and, having decided suddenly to return to Vancouver, Phillip had obviously thought there was no point in writing since a letter would likely be on the same train carrying him back to the coast. Had he thought of sending her a telegram? I could imagine him savouring the idea of surprising Harriet, waiting for her outside The Bay as she finished her shift, whisking her away to a café, planning the evenings they might spend together.

I reread the entry in Phillip's journal following his return to Vancouver.

March 21, 1917

Having been home now for a week, I take pen in hand with the hope—probably vain—that writing will help me to sort through the wreckage to which I have returned.

The clock in Old Grand's study has struck three. I have not been asleep and I think he heard me rummaging for something to read and pouring myself some port. In any event, I woke the nurse who'd been dozing in a chair outside his bedroom. Reluctantly, she let me peek in and I could see he was awake so I went in and spent a few minutes at his bedside. I believe he's forgotten that I've been in a few times to sit by him since my return, and he is still having great difficulty getting his words out but I think he was asking me why I'd come home. How I wish that I could talk to him about what matters. I couldn't though.

Per and Harriet have disappeared. From what I could understand from Mrs. Mezzkis, they will send a forwarding address, but for the time being she seems to be in quite a fog about their plans. She was fairly sure Per was going to look for work in the east and she thought he said something about Winnipeg but then he was talking about Montreal too. "How can you not be certain where they've gone?" I'm afraid I actually yelled at the woman which only made her angry and, even though much of what she said was in bombastic Lithuanian, I was able to understand some of the vile things she had to say about Harriet who has, I believe, suffered an accident, lost a baby, and ruined Mrs. Mezzkis's hall carpet. My child I must believe.

My child. It seems impossibly strange to see those two words recorded, inscribed on this page as words are chiselled onto a small gravestone.

My child.

I seem to remember Hat talking about a great-uncle some-where on the prairies. Was it Winnipeg? I wish I'd paid closer attention. I know that she will get in touch with me at the first opportunity and have wired the housekeeper at Malthus House to let me know if there is any contact made with Toronto, but I despair at Mrs. Frangobellocco doing anything more than receiving the cable and adding it to the growing mound of mail in the library. I am torn between catching the next train back and waiting for word to reach me here.

I have spent the days since my arrival tracking down Harriet's co-workers at The Bay and, of course, Elva and Myrtle. They seemed the most likely among the musicians to know anything about her whereabouts. It appears Per collected her pay at work and was his usual taciturn self, saying only that he and Harriet couldn't wait to get out of this "rotten sinkhole." Elva and Myrtle managed to visit her in the hospital, but they were neither of them very friendly to me, noting more than once, for my benefit, how weak and distraught Harriet was. When they went to visit her a second time, she had been discharged. It was a day before they got down to Cordova Street to Per's rooms only to find Mrs. Mezzkis readying them for new tenants.

Evenings I have been hanging out in places where I suspect Per went to drink with his dockfront buddies. They have been terrible, sluggish evenings, and I feel like someone who has been watching himself as a poor player in his own nightmare. Per, it seems, has made his specific plans known to no one. Last night concluded with a hellish episode on Georgia. As I headed home, I came upon an altercation between police and druggers that ended with the police chief being killed as well as a child being shot and dying on the street. Before police ushered us away, my eyes were lacerated with the image of that boy curled foetally on the unforgiving pavement, the end of a small trail of blood. I couldn't help thinking of another child, of another's blood.

CHAPTER 11

"**I**T WAS A LONG TRIP," AUNT HARRIET SAID, " THAT journey to Montreal. Every minute seemed marked with a peculiar combination of what?— speed and lethargy—that a train in motion has."

I tried to visualize the two of them in their coach seats, banked with blankets. Per with a bottle of whiskey hidden in with their lunch; Harriet's copy of *Tess of the D'Urbervilles* resting open against the star-patterned quilt. The slow hours; the countless stops; coach windows revealing a geography of Canada, with its mountains and foothills and flat fields unfolding like a dance in slow motion.

"I thought I would never get to Toronto, but I drew strength as we left the prairies and got into the rocky stretches with the train caught between cliffs and sea-sized lakes. Finally we pulled into Ottawa. It is while we were stopped there and Papa had gone off in search of a bottle of whiskey that I asked the conductor how much longer it would be before we reached Toronto. That's when I found out Toronto wasn't on the line to Montreal.

"Can you imagine?" she said. "Somehow in my mind was the notion that everything in Canada—all the major cities—lay along one line. Frantically I tried to think of some way to get Per to change his plans and detour through Toronto. When he got back to the station I could see he'd been successful getting his whiskey and was in a good mood. I broached the notion of going to Toronto but he just snorted and said, 'Are you crazy?' Our tickets were for Montreal and that's where we were going. I didn't think I could get back on the train. Per, I remember, half carried me.

"'I want to go home,' I kept crying and Per had his big arms wrapped around me, the way he sometimes did when I was a little girl, and he kept crooning, 'We'll find a home, *kjaere en*, we'll find us a home.'

"They say when you're lost it's best to simply stay put and wait for searchers to find you. I knew at that point I think that I should have done anything but leave Vancouver. It would have been better to have stayed and found a cheap room somewhere, or offered to do chores for Mrs. Mezzkis in return for my board, or asked Elva and Myrtle to put me up for a while. I think my boss at the music department in The Bay would have let me stay with his family even though it would have crowded them. All of these thoughts kept playing and replaying in my mind as the train pulled out of Ottawa and I saw the distance between Phillip and me growing with every mile of track."

As she talked about the trip east, Aunt Harriet's clenched hand beat against her thigh. "I should have stayed in Vancouver," she repeated. "Sometimes a single mistake, a lapse in judgment, can haunt us for a lifetime."

HER MEMORIES OF MONTREAL WERE SKETCHY. PER WAS able to find rooms for them in a boarding house close to the river docks.

"I had a bit of money saved that Per didn't know about," Aunt Harriet told me. "Our landlord had a telephone and, by giving him money in advance, I was allowed to use it to make a long distance call to Toronto. There was no answer. I tried several times over a period of days, although I could see it was trying the patience of the landlord and his wife.

"Finally someone picked up the phone—a house-keeper I guess—she spoke very broken English. I had trouble making out what she was saying and then it sank in. She was telling me that Phillip had gone back to Vancouver. I remember standing in that small, cramped parlour, the telephone earpiece in my hand for a min-ute, a couple of boarders watching me. I think Per and I were one of their favourite topics of discussion and my despair over this telephone call would create all kinds of speculation.

"I got my coat and went outside. I must have walked for about two hours. I have no idea where I went. Ended up in a little restaurant of some sort. There was a young man sitting at one of the tables nursing a coffee and, Curtis, I could see he was so in love with the waitress. His eyes never seemed to leave her and, when she'd brought me my coffee, she went over and sat with him and they were holding hands.

"I think I didn't actually cry until that point. I tried not to make myself obvious, but in a few minutes she came back over to my table with the coffee pot, and after refilling my cup, she reached out the way a mother does with a child, gave me a quick reassuring squeeze of the arm, without even looking.

"It's odd how the smallest of gestures can remain with us. There are parts of those first weeks in Montreal that are blocked out—I have no memory of them— but the fleeting pressure of a stranger's fingers ... I do remember trying to call the Pariston house in Vancouver a couple of times, always getting Edwina who was sugary sweet, promising to relay my messages to Phillip. And, of course, I kept writing, letter after letter, but nothing came in return."

The sense of being cut adrift, when she and Per settled in Montreal, was overwhelming, Aunt Harriet told me, but a full appreciation of what she felt was something to which I could not truly relate until I went to Vancouver to begin my studies at the Vancouver School of Art in the fall of 1965, where homesickness crept in often, like the evening fog. I knew no one in the city but there were locations that seemed familiar because Aunt Harriet had described them to me as places where she and Phillip spent time together. I found comfort visiting them—the walkways beneath the branches of ancient trees in Stanley Park, the sandy stretches of the public beach on English

Bay, Chinatown, the quirky streets just back from the dockyards.

"I think of the calls of the seagulls, and the horns of the boats," Aunt Harriet told me one time when I asked her about the impressions of Vancouver that stayed in her mind. "And the sound of machinery from the dockyards. If you were sad, these sounds and the soft air seemed to wrap themselves around you in a kind of ..." I recall her pausing, searching in the darkness for a word. "Sympathy," she said. "Sympathy."

The air was soft, I thought, softer than Alberta air. And the sounds were still there, the scraping cry of the gull, the shuttling of machinery, although now there was the intermittent, restless noise of traffic moving along busy streets close by. When I walked along Cordova Street, I tried to imagine the rooming house, now gone, where Harriet and Per had a small upper suite. "An ugly building with odd bits of gingerbread trim that didn't seem to quite fit," Aunt Harriet described it. "Stuck in between a warehouse and a hotel. The walls were a colour that made me think of cream that has been left out and formed a skin."

I found the block along East Georgia where the shooting had occurred which Phillip came upon as he headed home. Often I wished I had Phillip's journal in hand and I think it was while I was in Vancouver that winter the idea came to me to see if I might get it copied. Later, on return visits to the coast city, I sometimes took the copy with me, pulling it out to read as I soaked up some sun on Kitsilano Beach or sat on a park bench along English

Bay at my favourite time there, late afternoon, looking up from Phillip's careful penmanship at people walking their dogs or dashing into the water for a last swim of the day. Sometimes I stayed, the closed copy in my hands, as twilight set in, large cargo ships hedged against the horizon, lights in the Vancouver windows beginning to flirt with their reflections in the still water.

When I read Phillip's accounts of those days following his return home in March 1917, I sensed his restless spirit sometimes as I stood on a particular corner or sat on one of the barnacled rocks down from the seawall. I have never been a person who believed in ghosts but I think it is possible for the human mind to summon something close to a palpable presence and, at times, it seemed I caught a glimpse of him out of the corner of my eye, a figure hunched into his despair and loneliness.

March 29, 1917

I am convinced Harriet will be trying to contact me in Toronto. Mrs. Frangobellocco is as apt to ignore the phone as answer it and she never does anything more with the mail than gather it and pile it on the library table, so I hope my telegram to the post office is effective in getting my mail forwarded here. I wish Radcliffe were returning as originally scheduled but he is following up his New Orleans excursion with a stopover of two or three weeks in New York.

It seems wisest to stay here for the time being. If there is no contact in the next few days, I shall see if I can convince Dads to hire a detective. I wish Old Grand were not ill—he would do it without hitting me with a barrage of questions. My fear is that Hat has been very ill (even allowing for Elva's tendency toward dramatic exaggeration) and Per has been most foolhardy in making her travel.

I get out as much as I can. Edwina tries my patience. Whenever she finds me by myself she connives, within minutes, to plant one of her claws on my hand or arm as she launches into some profound dissertation on what was meant to be, or things working out for the best. I want to say: Edwina, some- times things work out for the worst and that's what's happened, and you're not making it one whit better.'

ON ONE OF MY TRIPS TO VANCOUVER IN THE LATE 1960S, Walter came with me. We took a room in an old hotel on English Bay. I had registered in a two-week summer drawing lab at the School of Art. Walter was devoting his days to developing a seamless tan at Wreck Beach. Before leaving Edmonton, at the last minute I'd thrown into the trunk of Walter's reconditioned Volvo the small wicker case in which I'd begun keeping all of the Pariston papers. One evening I spread the scraps of Phillip's sketches out, taking some kind of satisfaction placing them haphaz- ardly amongst my own sketches from the lab.

Walter was particularly intrigued by my conté renderings of the male nude. The school's models that summer included gymnasts and actors and one engi- neering student from UBC picking up some extra cash. Our drawing instructor had come close to apologizing for their handsome faces and bodies. There was still a sense among those who taught life drawing that "life" should mean something less than idyllic and I remembered our male models the winter I'd been taking classes had been a somewhat overweight middle-aged man who'd done some boxing in his youth and a grandfatherly bearded fellow who liked to tell us that he had once modelled for Man Ray.

Walter whistled at my sketches of the summer models and compared them with the ones Phillip had done half a century earlier. "You have similar styles," he noted. "If a person didn't already know; if you couldn't tell by the freshness of the paper, it would be hard to say which of you had done a lot of these." Walter sprawled on the rug in a state of near-nudity himself. The lamplight in our hotel bedroom leant a golden cast to his tan. He ran his finger along the line of a torso I had worked on that afternoon and I was reminded of Myron Evington and the way he had traced parts of the drawings I'd made in those first sketchbooks I'd kept.

In truth, I'd developed a style, a way of building mass with small curved strokes and sparse cross-hatching that was increasingly similar to Phillip's, although Phillip's drawings themselves were likely very much in the mode of his instructors.

There were fragments from four nudes among Harriet's papers. The footless male was the most complete. Another fragment revealed the upper torso of a woman, shoulders, breasts, the stomach to the navel. Aunt Harriet? I wondered. She said he'd sketched her often in their last few weeks together. Sometimes clothed; sometimes nude. He had made a habit of pinning the clothed sketches to the bedroom wall, though, and when that part of the house burned, those were all lost. The fragments came from the loose papers in his portfolio, papers caught by the wind.

The other two nudes were male, part of a lower back, and a torso from a side view. These three male nudes, I surmised, were among those Phillip worked on when he was in Toronto. Radcliffe Malthus belonged to a small circle that sketched, painted, and photographed the nude, a tiny eddy among stronger currents that would lead to the formation of the Group of Seven and a distinct Canadian style in which figure studies played no part at all.

The Toronto entries were ones that Aunt Harriet rarely asked me to read, but on that first visit to Vancouver, I read them aloud to Walter as we sipped gin and tonics, our window open to the soft Vancouver night, our room scattered with Phillip's sketches, my sketches.

March 2, 1917

Radcliffe took me, for the second time, to lunch at the Arts and Letters Club. It was a bon voyage for his New Orleans trip. We sat with other artists and conversation bubbled with remembrances of sketching excursions, and plans for forthcoming ones. They are a close group, these landscape artists, feeding off each other's enthusiasms. Radcliffe seems to be most friendly with Lawren Harris who comes from a family that has made a fortune in machinery.

When it was ascertained that there was a pianist in their midst, I was asked to play a few tunes. I chose some short pieces by

Chopin that I had committed to memory. As I played the "Tristesse Etude," one of the artists, a tall lanky fellow named Thomson—Tom Thomson—draped himself over the piano and, when I finished, asked if I knew "Annie Laurie." Before long the piano was surrounded and we were engaged in a full-scale singalong.

Thomson, at the start of the lunch, seemed quiet and rather taciturn—especially when the conversation turned to talk of events in Europe—it seems he failed his medical too. But, as the afternoon wore on and he got a few drinks under his belt, and exercised his voice with singing, he became more talkative. Started calling me "kid" and invited me to his studio to see what he's working on. Harris, when he found out I am determined to be an artist myself, encouraged me to go and have a tour of the Studio Building. Radcliffe's eye had been caught earlier by a young waiter, and he declined to join us.

Thomson is an interesting chap. He lives in a little shack back of Harris's Studio Building. Quite amazing, really, like something you might find in the backwoods. But then there is a fine backwoods quality to him. He showed me a number of oil sketches he has made on location, one of which he is now developing into a large-scale painting. I admired the sketches. They are raw, but somehow incredibly vibrant and honest. Perhaps these are the new terms for a Canadian landscape—none of your British effeteness or varnished Dutch pieces. I kept wondering if I might find some equivalency in painting the figure—which interests me more than the shorelines of Algonquin Park.

"You should come out to the park, kid," he said, when we had done a fair amount of damage to a bottle of whiskey he keeps at hand alongside his turpentine. "Greatest thing, getting out there and sketching from a canoe. Fishing's good too."

Apparently he goes there to work as a guide following spring breakup. He says for me to let him know when I can come up and he'll set aside a few days for a sketching trip. The prospect is appealing.

He insisted that I take with me one of the sketches I admired. I have it before me now. There are evergreens of indigo and purple, darkened with black, wedged against poplar and birch in autumn golds and oranges—everything underlined with the clear green of a river or lake. Very striking. It is odd—the kinship I feel for this man, and, indeed, the excitement I feel for what is happening in Toronto.

I have joined Radcliffe's Wednesday group which meets in his studio to work from models, and that is invigorating in itself. So much better than drawing from plaster casts.

"I AGREE WITH THAT," WALTER SAID. "FLESH OVER plaster."

I closed the journal.

"Why do people do it?" Walter drained the last of his gin and tonic and fished a nearly-melted ice cube out of the bottom of his glass and ran it over his chest.

"What?"

"You know. Draw naked people."

"Why do people do anything?" For some reason I felt Walter's words as an attack against myself. "Anything beyond satisfying their needs for food, shelter, and clothing? I think artists draw the human figure because they are intrigued. The way we're put together; the way the world is put together; the way the two fit together …" My words sounded slurred. "It's a kind of mystery. Intriguing."

"Okay," Walter giggled, getting up and loping around the room, careful not to step on any of the sketches with his bare feet. "That's a good answer." He added a couple of ice cubes to his glass and splashed the last of the gin over them. "Oops," he said. "You like another?"

I shook my head and began picking up the sketches.

"But I think it's a kind of foreplay," he added, looking at me out of the corner of his eye. "Drawing nude people is sexy. Skin against a blanket, a bit of wall, the floor, a chair. All the parts we make love with, eyes that have looked into lovers' eyes, lips, cock ..."

It was in my mind to challenge him. I knew Walter's enjoyment, at times, of baiting me. But I knew too that there was some truth in what he said, one of those truths that skittered around the edge of anything I was prepared to deal with.

"What about someone like Tom Thomson then? Who only painted lakeshore trees. Are you saying he was asexual, or do you think there's foreplay in something like a jack pine being buffeted by a west wind?"

"It's a possibility," Walter said. "I mean that he found a kind of sexual stimulation in painting from nature."

I shook my head. "He was asexual. His love was painting; his energy was painting. He had nothing left over."

"Wasn't he found dead in the water with his pants unbuttoned?"

"Oh for Christ's sake ..."

"I'm taking a shower." Walter slipped out of his shorts, stretched, and headed for the bathroom.

I felt the gin spinning me toward the double bed I'd claimed nearest the door.

PHILLIP ENCOUNTERED THOMSON ONCE MORE BEFORE the artist headed out to Algonquin Park in early April but the account of his visit to Canoe Lake and the time spent there has been lost in the pages excised from the journal. I asked Aunt Harriet if she had any idea why May and June had been removed from the diary with what would appear to have been a razor blade.

"I've wondered that myself," she said. "Jean noticed that there were a number of pages that had been carefully sliced out when she first read it. I think that woman who was reading it to me in the hospital saw details she didn't like and removed those pages, although it seems like a petty thing to have done.

"He did go to the park and spend some time with Thomson. I remember him telling me about it. But the weather hadn't been very good, and mostly they were in a lodge there. Phillip had brought a couple of bottles of the whiskey Thomson favoured, and he said the artist could get quite touchy after a certain point. Phillip went out in the rain to get away from an argument between Thomson and the man who ran the lodge.

"It seems to me it was while he was at the lodge that the cable came calling him back to Vancouver when his grandfather took a turn for the worse."

On one of those pieces of scarred paper there is what appears to be a sketch of a pine tree. Noticeable is a sinuous quality to the configuration of the branches that makes me think of Thomson's large canvases, a kind of art nouveau gracefulness. I like to think that Phillip made the sketch with Thomson at his side or close by. Perhaps there had been a break in the rain, allowing them out for a few hours. I can imagine the two lanky figures with their sketching materials, working quietly, intent on capturing the patterns before them. Thomson and "the kid."

The Thomson painting Aunt Harriet had inherited from Phillip more by point of possession than anything else had helped to build in me an abiding curiosity about this man who was not actually one of the Group of Seven but a key player in the movement that would lead to its formation.

Phillip's instructor for the few months he was in Toronto in 1917 was J.Y. Spangler, a middle-aged man who made his living primarily by portraiture, but who conducted lessons out of his studio. His paintings of university chancellors and Ontario politicians can be found scattered through the hallways of a number of institutions. They are competent if not compelling.

One though, of an art gallery patroness, has a flatness to its planes—the oversized bell-shaped hat, the fall of a fur wrap over the shoulder and arm, the panels of a green dress—that seems in sympathy with what Thomson and his landscape artists were creating. The negative spaces in oyster greys and blues move assertively against a red outlining of the figure that, when I first saw a print of it, made me think of Thomson's *The West Wind*, a painting he'd completed just before his death. The pine in the foreground is stylized, its branches sinuously connected to

flat planes of dark green, outlined in red against a scud-
ding sky and lake of blues, greens, and whites.

In one of his journal entries, Phillip briefly wrote of
both Spangler and Thomson.

April 20, 1917

*I am back in Toronto—since Wednesday. The house seems very
empty without Radcliffe and his friends. No mail has come from
Hat, although, when I quizzed Mrs. Frangobellocco, it seems a
woman did phone and ask for me one day. I have been checking
the harbourfront to see if I can spot Per among the stevedores
and warehouse workers. I expect Hat will telephone again soon
if she is in the city. Once more I am torn between staying in, in
case that happens, and going out and searching for them.*

*To keep my sanity I have recommenced my lessons with
Spangler. For two hours every other day I try to focus on nothing but the tasks he sets for me.*

*I found a note from Thomson in the pile of mail on the library
table, just a short message from Mowat Lodge reminding me that
I am welcome to join him in Algonquin. Again—a dilemma.*

*I asked Spangler if he had seen any of Thomson's paintings
and what he thought of them. He said he's been over to Harris's
Studio Building a few times and he admires what the artists
there are doing. Arched his shaggy eyebrows and said, while he
isn't one to enjoy painting out of doors, his own portraits and
still lifes are 'for the new century too.' Like Radcliffe, Spangler
is a creature of the town. A wire from Radcliffe tells me he will
be back in two weeks. I am sure the Wednesday Club will re-
assemble with his return, and look forward to that.*

I have decided to write Dads this evening and put aside the anger I've carried with me since his refusal to pay for a detective to search out Per and Harriet. By saving some each week from my allowance, I believe I will be able to do that on my own before long. Edwina, of course, is behind his refusal. She has been convincing him I'm sure that Harriet's departure was written in the stars and that her continued absence will be my reclamation.

IN MY ART HISTORY COURSE DURING MY YEAR AT THE Vancouver School of Art, I'd been able to do an independent study of Thomson even though the instructor was reluctant to stray from a curriculum that moved chronologically through the centuries. We were entrenched in the Byzantine period.

"I could look for a Byzantine influence in Thomson's painting," I had joked as I made the plea to do the study.

"You would do better to look at the Fauve artists," he said drily, "and imagine them mating with magazine illustrators. But you have my permission to do it."

I left our meeting with the resolve that I would show him Thomson had begun the forging of something unique in Canadian art. My instructor was right, of course. Thomson's paintings reveal the strong influence of art nouveau, its undulating lines and asymmetry having seeped into all aspects of popular culture, including the designs at the commercial studio where Thomson worked for years. I discovered in my research for the paper that some art historians thought Thomson was influenced (as were J.E.H. MacDonald and Lawren Harris) by a school of Scandinavian artists working in the Jugendstil style, a

Germanic application of art nouveau given to flat planes of colour and irregular forms with mountains and trees creating decorative motifs.

Critics were beginning to agree that Thomson's studio pictures, the ones he developed on large canvases during Toronto winters, were somewhat self-consciously art nouveau, while his sketches, painted on boards during trips into the Ontario wilderness, showed spontaneity and vigour. I wrote and asked Jean if she could arrange to have Aunt Harriet's painting photographed and send me a colour print. When it arrived, along with a short note dictated by Harriet expressing her pleasure in my interest in it, I pasted it into an appendix of prints attached to my paper.

Thomson had been eighteen years older than Phillip Pariston the year they died. My thoughts turned often, as I worked on my paper, to the possibilities of what Phillip might have accomplished if he had been given the gift of those extra years to keep working at his craft, of the directions he might have gone.

"Everyone's lives are filled with such ifs," Aunt Harriet had once said to me, and her voice circled my thoughts. "If ..."

July 19, 1917

I read today of Thomson's death at Canoe Lake. It is beyond belief. I cannot fathom him entangling himself in his fishing line and falling out of his canoe unless he were very drunk indeed, which seems unlikely at that time of day—if they have determined it correctly. With the war claiming so many, it is a particular jolt to realize that the world can be a dark and dangerous place even in the quiet wilderness of Algonquin, far removed from man-made mayhem.

Old Grand is somewhat better today. I think it is possible he recognized me, briefly.

"I THINK I WOULD HAVE LIKED THOMSON," WALTER decided, leafing through a biography of the artist. "A painter who likes to fish." We'd just been to the art gallery downtown and had spent some time looking at a Thomson in their permanent collection, one of his few paintings to include a figure. A man fishing.

"He had that kind of passion you find in truly committed artists. Like Van Gogh."

"Yeah, I know what you mean," Walter laughed. "I saw that movie about Van Gogh. Committed is a good word."

"A fine line between artistry and insanity? I wonder if Phillip had that kind of genius? He had a passion for being an artist, but I don't know if he had that kind of inner passion, or vision or world view—whatever you want to call it. Like Emily Carr or Lawren Harris. Almost re-inventing the world."

"Are you wondering if you have it?" Walter smiled slyly at me.

"I know I don't have it. Yet."

"I guess it's something you know when it's there."

"I'm not even sure that's it. I think maybe there's no awareness, that it's as unconscious, in a way, as breathing."

Walter looked at me quizzically. After leaving the gallery, we had drifted back to my apartment where I'd thrown together a salad, warmed up some lasagna, and uncorked a bottle of Chianti. As I finished putting away our dishes, he had flipped back in the diary to the last entry before the excised pages, and had begun reading aloud.

May 9, 1917

Radcliffe's Wednesday Group met for about four hours this afternoon. Our model was a young man who has been a farm labourer and is now odd-jobbing in the city. His muscles are well-defined and I can see Radcliffe is mesmerized by his mop of curly hair—among other things. I think he used up every photography plate he owned in the course of the afternoon.

I was pleased with the sketches I made, and the model, Andrew ("Call me 'Andy'") kept coming over to look at them every time we took a break. He seemed totally intrigued that I could lavish as much attention as I do in the process of creating his image. Radcliffe, I could see, was not amused so I whispered to Andy that if he wanted to do more sessions it would be to his benefit to hover around the man with the camera. He wet his lips and—

"THAT MUST BE WHERE IT'S RAZOR-BLADED OUT."

"Aunt Harriet thought it was a nun—or whatever she was—at the hospital. Probably read ahead in it when Aunt Harriet was sleeping."

"I'm not sure." Walter stretched out full length on the floor, trying to balance a wineglass on his stomach, which he felt was hardening to a coffee-table firmness from the swimming regimen he had been submitting himself to over the past six weeks.

"What do you mean?" I used the coffee table to rest my glass on, even though I had been going with Walter to the pool for the past month.

"I'm guessing, of course."

"What?"

"That your Phillip became involved with one of Radcliffe's young men."

"You're out of your mind."

Walter didn't say anything, just smiled at me with a maddening kind of smugness. A Haydn sonata on the phonograph, the music coming in small pounces and flights, danced around the idea.

"He was fucking the model," Walter insisted. "Or vice versa."

"But there's no—"

"What?"

"No indication. No reason to think ..."

"Phillip was probably as surprised as anyone else. It happens."

I studied Walter's face until he looked away from me, and—in the process of averting his gaze—spilled his wine.

"Shit," he said softly, pulling himself up and loping into the kitchen to get a dishcloth.

"He razored those pages out himself," Walter said, mopping up the spreading stain. "I'd better go. Geoff will be wondering where I am."

"Your accountant?"

"Well—maybe more than that." Walter grinned. "Don't raise your eyebrows at me, friend. There's a world out there—"

He didn't finish the sentence, just gave me a backward wave as he headed out the door.

CHAPTER 12

WALTER HAD DRIVEN ME TO SCHOOL FOR A couple of years until he was assigned a position in a new junior high across town. I didn't mind being back on the bus and I knew Walter enjoyed chauffeuring when we did go out after hours. In the year after Aunt Harriet died, he drove me every couple of weeks to visit Jean in the Sunset Arms.

Jean had a tiny room filled with houseplants and dominated by an oversized television tuned relentlessly to the soaps. With Aunt Harriet's passing, she seemed to allow herself to drift with whatever currents might flow through the course of her days, hyperdramatic strands of the TV shows, the arrival of a dinner tray, the visit of a nurse. Some days she didn't seem to know us but even on those days Walter discovered ways of engaging her, bringing us into her realm of attention.

"Hey, beautiful," he would say, bounding into the room ahead of me. "Whatcha up to?"

Generally Jean would look at him somewhat startled and it would take a few seconds for her to be won over by his wide smile.

"Not much," she'd say, her voice starchy and tiny.

"I don't believe you," Walter would tease. "I saw that new male nurse. Giorgio? That's his name, isn't it? You been making up to him?"

"Oh, you!" Jean would giggle into one hand while waving him away with the other scrawny claw.

She was failing quickly, though, and one afternoon as we sat with her, sharing tea and some pale, cardboard-like cookies for which she had developed a particular fondness, Walter managed to get her to talk about Phillip Pariston's journal.

"She'd have me reading it all right. Just about every night. I didn't think it was proper then—the words of the dead. It wasn't right somehow ..."

"Not right?"

"Being so personal. 'I'm not reading that, Harriet,' I'd say. 'It would embarrass his spirit.' But then I'd look at her, poor wounded thing, and you couldn't be denying her." Jean lost herself for a few minutes in the retrieval of cookie crumbs over the front of her housecoat.

"There were parts you didn't like to read?" I knew that Aunt Harriet found Jean a reluctant reader, someone who managed to torture the written word, but I hadn't thought of her reluctance being connected to anything more than a sense that it was something she did poorly.

"I didn't like to read none of it. Spooky, that's what I thought. She used to get others to read it aloud sometimes. Just a couple of people though. Them she trusted. At Mrs. Carter's there was that piano player. I think he was a little bit in love with Harriet. Sometimes he'd come early just so they could have a visit."

"Early?"

"There'd be him on piano, Harriet with her fiddle and that Russian girl on an accordion. He'd come in the late afternoon, before they'd begin work."

I remembered Aunt Harriet mentioning having played at one of the boarding houses to help pay her keep. I'm pretty certain her exact words were, "Sometimes the survivors are not very nice people." When I pressed her to elaborate, she sighed and said something about smoothing away wrinkles left by unpleasant memories. The tactile nature of the image had struck me at the time.

"She was a tartar, that one. Emma Carter." Jean pursed her lips and shook her head. "She and Harriet had a scrap once—something to do with Harriet owing her board money—I thought the house would come apart. 'You give that back to me. It's mine.' I can hear her screaming to this day and I finally went up to Emma Carter's bedroom— she used it as her office—and it took everything I had in me to say it but I did. 'You quit tormenting that crippled girl,' I said. 'You give her back her book and papers. She ain't got a whole lot in the world and you can't keep them from her.'"

Jean had finished her tea and closed her eyes. Walter gently removed the cup from her lap and fixed a small wool blanket she sometimes used as a shawl more securely over her shoulders.

"'I got my baby, Jeannie,'" she whispered as Walter bent closer to her. "Harriet thought she was jealous— Emma Carter had no kids herself and she had no patience with babies. Except for Phip. 'I got my baby, Jeannie,' she used to say, 'and that's one thing Emma can never have.'"

Walter was quieter than usual as he drove me home, finally turning on the radio to a classical music station. His own family, I knew, had come from Ukraine just before the First World War and had their own story of difficult times.

"Must've been a hard time, being blind and pregnant. Trying to find a place to live and everything," he said, when there was a pause in the music. "It's hard to imagine. I suppose there was help."

"Even with all that happened, I think social assistance wasn't that easy to come by." I tried to bring to mind the few times Aunt Harriet had allowed me to edge into the territory of those years. "I believe Aunt Harriet stayed in two or three places before she finally met Uncle Hart. My family thinks she was in an asylum for a while. Maybe the YMCA? It was used as a home for those who remained in shock. There are gaps ..."

When Walter and I went to visit Jean a couple of weeks later, I formulated a list of questions in my mind, determined to find out more of what had happened in that period in Aunt Harriet's life from the time Phillip Pariston died until she met and married my uncle. I knew she had made an attempt or two to make contact with the

Paristons, but these efforts had been successfully blocked by Edwina. Hartley, she told me, she first met at a picnic.

"One of those big summery affairs with a brass band and children running through the park. It was very filled with sound. Lots of cheering as Hartley pitched a ball game. At one point Phip got away from me and ran out onto the playing field. Everyone laughed and, after the game, Hartley gave Phip a ball to play with. He had so much patience with children. Of course Phip wouldn't leave the poor man alone.

"To be desired ... to be valued—we take sustenance ... and Phip had grown so fond of him."

Jean seemed to have shrunk in size since our last visit, a small, wizened, birdlike creature enveloped in the blanket shawl.

"Hey, gorgeous." On her bureau, Walter placed a small bouquet he'd picked up at the last minute. "Some posies."

Our appearance seemed barely to register. I thought I saw her gaze edge, rather warily, to Walter's activity at the bureau.

"Gor'," she said. Or "Gord." The word rested in her throat, plaintive, lost.

"What'd you say, sweetie?" Walter found one of her hands and rubbed it gently. Jean looked up at him with a kind of wonder but without recognition.

"Gor'," she muttered and I noticed her cheeks were moist with tears.

Although she never again recognized us, we visited her for another four months. Then, shrunk to almost nothing, she died, a couple of days before spring break, and Walter and I delayed the trip we had been planning to the coast. We would have a few days less in Vancouver, but it seemed important to be among the few who gathered to sing "Rock of Ages," her favourite hymn, to drop roses onto the casket in the midst of March snow, to review the smattering of biographical information the minister had gleaned from who knew where, intoned to the sparse gathering at the funeral parlour. Born in Glasgow in 1894. Emigrated to Canada at age seventeen. Married Gordon Abercrombie before she turned twenty. Her husband killed in a mining accident within the first year of her marriage. Devoted her life to domestic service. Long-time employee and friend of the Coleman family. Staunch member of the First Presbyterian Church.

"She would have come over in 1911," I figured as Walter and I settled into a downtown lounge with a decent house wine to plan our trip. "It's funny but I find it hard to think of her having a life apart from Aunt Harriet. It's like she was just—always there. Even when she mentioned her sister or her church, it was as if they were—I don't know—stuff tucked away in storage somewhere. Aunt Harriet was her house and home."

"I think you need another glass of wine." Walter smiled. With the late afternoon sunlight and its slight promise of spring filtering through the blinds of the bar, we toasted Jean Abercrombie.

CHAPTER 13

THEY HAD COME ACROSS THE OCEAN AS YOUNG people, part of those waves of settlement we had studied in an abstract way in our grade five social studies at Yarrow Elementary. Jean Abercrombie. Harriet and Per. Phillip and Everett with their father and grandfather. Edwina. Radcliffe Malthus, about whom I thought of often, frustrated by the scar of missing pages ridged along the gutter of Phillip Pariston's journal, a scar I had replicated with a seam of quick-drying glue in my photocopy.

Aunt Harriet had little to say about Malthus.

"Phillip didn't talk much about his days in Toronto," she told me once when I asked. "And when I lived there, it was in a very different world from his."

He did tell her about the time he spent with Thomson, his trip to Algonquin Park. She remembered he sometimes propped the Canoe Lake oil painting against the back of her bureau where it could be easily seen whether you were in bed or in the sitting room. And he'd shown her his favourites from a portfolio of drawings he'd done for his art instructor. But he hadn't talked about those actual days, those lengthening days of spring melting into summer.

"My feeling is that it was too painful for him to revisit them, I think it was the most lonely time in his life. He was cut off from his family—and my letters weren't getting through to him. When he was called home to be with Old Grand, I think he was relieved to go."

At the time I agreed with Aunt Harriet, but now Walter's hypothesis about Phillip and those lost weeks niggled at me. When I finally had a chance to go to Toronto in 1978, I decided to find out what I could about his time there. And I was determined, too, to discover more about Radcliffe Malthus.

The opportunity came up when an ad in *Canadian Art* magazine offered a weeklong summer institute organized around collections in the Art Gallery of Ontario. For the busy schedule of that week, I'd decided to stay with the study group in residence at the University of Toronto. But I added a few days onto the end of the course and booked a room in an inexpensive hotel off Yonge Street close to downtown. It would be possible to walk along some of the same streets Phillip Pariston had walked along during the months he lived at Malthus House. Visit the mansion, I hoped—enter rooms where he might have worked on sketches, sipped coffee, read novels from Old Grand's reading list, sifted through the clutter of mail in search of a letter from Aunt Harriet.

I found myself almost giddy with the prospect. But,

since it was April when I registered, over three months of waiting loomed. There were things, though, I could do in Edmonton to prepare for the trip. Many days, after work, I made my way over to the Rutherford Library and into a reading room which offered access to an archive of Canadian newspapers on microfiche. Perhaps Radcliffe Malthus would serve as some kind of a key to those lost pages in Phillip Pariston's journal.

When had Malthus died? In *Canadian Who's Who* volumes from the 1930s there were entries for the photographer but he was absent from the 1939 edition. It seemed like a place to start and so I delved into the obituaries in edition after edition of 1939's *The Globe and Mail*. Finally in a March weekend paper, I found it—not only his obituary but an article.

In the photo that accompanied the article, Malthus peered with a bemused arrogance at the camera. He looked like he might have been about sixty, so it would have been taken some twenty years before his death. A thin moustache, probably dyed to an assertive blackness, played across his upper lip. There was a studied elegance to his clothes—a felt hat with its brim angled across his forehead, a dark vest and jacket with a handkerchief spilling from its pocket, a white shirt with a stiff collar and a houndstooth-patterned bow tie.

Pioneer Photographer Malthus Dies

After a brief illness, pioneer photographer Radcliffe Eugene Malthus died in his Rosedale home, March 20th. A prominent figure in the city's art scene over the past several decades, Malthus left his house to the city with the proviso that it be maintained as a drawing and photography studio. A gallery in Malthus House will be devoted to a display of the photographer's work including portraits of three prime ministers and his award-winning beach series which features Torontonians, over many years, at the lakeside during the hottest days of summer.

Malthus was born in Manchester, England in 1861. His father, Alexander Malthus, was a chief partner in the Western Shipping Line. His mother, Eugenia Pariston Malthus, was a landscape artist of some note in the Manchester area. After attending Cambridge briefly, Radcliffe Malthus sailed to the United States and enrolled at the Pennsylvania Academy of the Fine Arts where he studied under the noted Philadelphia artist Thomas Eakins. He settled in Toronto in 1893 where he designed and built Malthus House over a period of two years. The photography and art studio of Malthus House became a centre for artists and musicians. Malthus was also a staunch supporter of the Arts and Letters Club. Apart from the photography displayed at Malthus House, his photographs have been acquired by several galleries across Canada. His nieces, Edith Bircombe and Mrs. Harold Garrison, Malthus's heirs, have plans to issue a collection of the photographs as a limited edition pictorial album.

THE LIBRARY HAD TELEPHONE BOOKS FOR CANADA'S major cities. It seemed like a long shot, looking up his nieces, but there was a listing under Bircombe, E. in the Toronto directory—nothing for Garrison. Too late to call that evening, but I dialed her number as soon as I finished work the next day. I thought I heard the sound of laboured breathing before a whispery voice answered, "Yes?"

"Edith Bircombe?"

Another wheeze.

I explained my mission.

She acknowledged her Malthus kinship. When I asked if it would be possible to meet with her or her sister at the end of July, there was a short, gasping pause.

"Louella?"

"Mrs. Garrison," I said.

"Louella's been dead for thirty years."

When I gave her more of the particulars of my connection to her uncle, nebulous as it sounded, she agreed to see me.

"Call me when you get to Toronto."

My thanks and goodbye seemed to get lost in a series of small, animal-like coughs.

I HADN'T SEEN MUCH OF WALTER THE WEEKS I WAS dashing off to the Rutherford Library to prepare for my trip to Toronto. And I don't think I realized how much I missed our get-togethers until he called me on a Saturday morning in June and suggested we meet for dinner at a café we frequented at the south end of the High Level Bridge. He sounded down—not his usual self.

I arrived first and managed to get a favourite window seat where there was a good interior view of consignment paintings and, outside, activity on a sidewalk we had often walked along ourselves years earlier as we studied to become teachers. Students, between sessions

now, in summer garb, enjoying the June weather, some
on bicycles.

I could see the parking lane in behind the Garneau
Theatre and saw Walter's car pull in. Surprisingly for someone of his height, after his old Volvo died, he always drove
small, sporty cars. I found pleasure watching him emerge
like some kind of compact toy unfolding upon release. As
he walked to the café, he worked at loosening cramped
muscles, arching his head back, rotating his shoulders. He
spotted me at the window and smiled. I waved.

"Curt-boy." He clasped my shoulder as he sat down.

"How are you?" I calculated that, unusual for us, we
hadn't got together for a meal for three weeks.

"Oh—you know." He rubbed a hand across his mouth
and then made a mock-goofy face. "Visiting the dumps."

A waiter who could have doubled for Robert Redford
took our wine order.

I waited until he was gone before I said anything.

"The dumps?"

Walter, with his large farm-boy hands, played with
his napkin for a minute and then shrugged. "This time I
think I'm the dumpee."

"Your accountant? I thought ..."

"Go figure." This made him laugh.

"Do you want to talk—?"

"No. I want to drink."

Robert Redford returned with a carafe of Merlot and
took our meal orders. Wine poured, we hoisted our glasses
and I filled him in on my summer plans for Toronto and
the research I'd been doing at the library.

"It never fades, does it? Thoughts about your aunt and her handsome lover boy." He gave his head a single shake that he seemed to have developed solely as a comment on what he sometimes called my Pariston trance.

"I suppose so, but also Tom Thomson, the Group of Seven ..."

"Ah, yes. Your world of art and artists."

"You seem to be at loose ends. You should come with me."

He ran a hand over his forehead and pushed back a stray lock of hair. I couldn't help thinking of that accountant—what was his name?—Geoff?—running his hands over that same territory—hair, forehead, lips ...

Walter raised his eyebrows. "You're blushing."

"Just a bit hot in here." I managed a small laugh. "Seriously. You should think about it. Accommodations already booked."

"It's a thought."

We tackled our meals and, when we were finished, Walter beckoned the waiter. "Two Drambuies and one bread pudding to share."

"Oh, lord." I patted my stomach.

"I would come," he said, "but the time you've booked is right when I promised my sister I'd help her organize a family reunion."

"Something major?"

"Mandriuks from all over the prairie provinces and some cousins from the Maritimes. Who ever thought there'd be Ukrainians settling in New Brunswick?"

Our liqueurs and dessert arrived. I raised my glass of Drambuie. "To the Slavic invasion."

CHAPTER 14

MY ROOM IN ONE OF THE COLLEGE DORMITORIES at U of T was spartan and lacked air conditioning but I spent as little time in it as possible. The Institute's instructors were in summer mode, doing what they could to bring some humour to their sessions, and among the registrants, we quickly formed a group determined to check out restaurants and watering holes every evening. Whenever I had a free daytime hour, I often hurried over to spend more time at the Art Gallery with its impressive collections. Thomson's *The West Wind* drew me back time and again. It had been hard to gauge the size of the painting from the reproductions in books and posters. Quite different from the small painting I owned (I'd packed the colour photocopy with me) but mesmerizing in its size and force despite what critics might say about it being an homage to art nouveau.

Towards the end of the institute, I missed a late afternoon lecture on Henry Moore's sculptures to meet Phip for a drink in the trendy lounge of an old brick hotel close to the advertising firm where he worked. I hadn't called him until midweek and it turned out he would be headed out on holidays to a summer cottage in the Gatineau hills on Friday.

"Noreen's been up there for the last week and Dana and her husband are coming in from Ottawa on the weekend with the baby—Connor."

He pulled photos from his inside jacket pocket. Most of the pictures were of the newborn, but in one I could see that Phip's oldest daughter had settled into a resemblance of her grandmother, an echo of the angular face, the thick blond hair.

"How does it feel to be a grandfather?"

A waiter arrived with our drinks. He was lithe, vested, chatty in a way that could only help raise the ante on a tip.

"Dana reminds me of your mother," I said, savouring the medicinal iciness of my gin and tonic. "The way she looked in those photos of her when she was a young woman."

"Definitely Scandinavian," Phip agreed, sampling his scotch. "The baby's wonderful. I'm beginning to believe all the advertising copy I've ever written about the subject. How about you? Bona fide bachelor?"

"That's me."

"A good companion."

I looked at him questioningly.

"I mean a companion to the ladies. You must have found someone after Mom died, someone to hash over the concerts, talk about the latest books, what's up in the galleries."

This time I could feel a sudden heat come to my own cheeks.

Phip chuckled. "A playboy. Never mind. I still appreciate the time you spent with her those last years. She wasn't always easy to be around."

"I loved being with her. In some ways I think it was the best time of my life."

"Still poring over her scraps of paper, her keepsakes?"

"It still intrigues me. I thought I might write it up in some way."

"Hey." Phip raised his glass to a toast position. "Go for it. I know Dana—well, probably Amber too—would like to see the result. When they were teenagers they got it all out and listened to the copies of the tapes you made before Mom died. I think Dana did a school project. High school?—or maybe grade nine."

I pushed the twist of lime into my drink. It was the time for plunges. "Have you ever checked out any of Phillip Pariston's Toronto connections?"

"Not really." Phip lit a cigarette and settled back. In his tie and summer suit, he seemed part of a club of prosperous businessmen who had quickly filled the small lounge. White collar men with a heftiness kept in check by memberships to fitness centres. "I went and saw the Thomson stuff that's been going up in the galleries, of course. There was quite a bit of it on display even when Mom and Dad lived here. Mom liked me to describe the places to her."

"And Radcliffe Malthus?"

"The photographer?"

"I'm anxious to find out more about him. Next week I think I might be able to meet up with his niece. He was an important person in your father's life."

"My father? You think so?" Phip paused for a moment, started to say something, then changed his mind.

"I remember when Malthus died. That was before the war." Phip loosened his tie and sighed. "I must have been about twenty then. Remember reading the newspaper announcement to Mom."

"Had they ever met?"

Phip shook his head. "No, I don't think so. I went to Malthus House once, though, with a buddy who had a leave before going overseas, a guy from Manitoba who'd been studying architecture, and Mom made us tell her all about the house. It'd been fixed up into kind of a museum with photos all over the place. We thought Casa Loma was more interesting, though."

"I'm planning to get over to Malthus House. When the course is finished."

"It's actually not far from here." Phip played with the ice left in his glass, wetting his fingers, the long Ahlstrom fingers, and rubbing the moisture against the back of his neck. "There's probably a pamphlet on him."

I walked Phip to his car parked in a lot a couple of blocks away.

"So things are really okay with you?" he said, searching his pockets for car keys. There was a touch of concern in his voice that drifted on the patness of what people say to one another in moments of parting.

"Everything's fine." The words emerged over a small, nervous laugh that I hadn't intended. "Life is good."

"You know, we're fortunate to live in a settled time." Phip left the door open as he eased himself into the seat and turned on the air conditioning. "You'll never have to go to war. I don't think my daughters' husbands will, or—we can hope—little Connor. Is it just luck? I hope no one in the family ever has to go through what Mom went through. There were times when everything would double back on her and she'd be crazy with grief and remembrance. All the worlds that crumbled around her."

"I know." I ran my fingers along the top of the car door. "We are lucky."

"You take care." He reached out for a final handshake. "Hope you find what you're looking for."

BEFORE I LEFT EDMONTON I HAD TRACKED DOWN EDITH Bircombe's address and sent her a note reminding her of my desire to see her when I was in Toronto. Once the Institute was over, I followed up with a phone call and, in that whispery voice she agreed to an afternoon meeting.

She lived in a walk-up off Church Street, a fading, stucco edifice with some Romanesque touches and hints of stained glass here and there in windows that had escaped replacement. I was not surprised to find her attached to an oxygen canister. She was an aging butterfly, layered in bright silk that had, at some point, been subjected to a batik process that left trails through fields of maroon and crimson and celery green. She gestured me in and beckoned for me to follow her as she trundled the oxygen canister into a sitting room rampant with cushions that looked as if they might have been fashioned from the remains of the garment she wore.

"I'm an artist too," she whispered. "I work in silk."

"Very ... nice," I managed.

"Sooo ..." she said, once she had settled into an arm-chair and manoeuvred the canister into position. "You're looking into the life of Radcliffe Malthus." She giggled faintly. "He's not remembered much any more. I think his photographs are in storage at the National Gallery at the moment. You asked about Louella. That's a portrait of the two of us." She waved to a framed photograph across the room.

I got up to take a closer look. They were teenagers, these girls, dressed in a flapper style that made me think of photographs of Clara Bow or Louise Brooks. Bee-stung lips, bobbed hair, eyebrows refashioned with a makeup pencil. Filmy silk and pearls.

"He sent one of those photos to Hollywood," she mused. "Louella and I thought they might be looking for more sisters—you know, like the Gishes, but no one ever responded. I guess there were so many. But then, Mary Pickford came from Toronto. People have to come from somewhere and why not Toronto?" She flashed a lipstick-stained smile at me that crumpled into a gasp-ing spell that sent her fingers scuttling over valves in the breathing apparatus.

"Emphysema," she explained, regaining her breath. "Louella died a couple of years after the war. Traffic acci-dent. She was Rad's favourite, I think, although he was always very sweet to me. Pour yourself a drink." She waved to a mahogany cabinet, one of the few pieces of furniture that remained silk-free.

"Can I get you something?"

"Absinthe," she said. "I shouldn't, but ..."

The cabinet contained a jumble of bottles and decanters. "In the corner."

I found what I imagined to be the fabled drink of Beaudelaire, Rimbaud, and Hemingway—not to mention the poison of choice for a host of impressionist painters.

"I thought it was impossible to get hold of absinthe nowadays," I said.

"Difficult," she wheezed, "but not impossible."

I poured myself a drink of Madeira.

"Louella would dress up like a young man and go to his parties." She took a butterfly sip of the absinthe. "He seemed to like that."

"Do you have more of his photos?" I asked.

"Oh, heavens yes," she laughed. "You go and look in the study. The walls are lined. And there's a boxful or two. You can look at those."

"Did you know him well?"

"Not really well. Louella and I were born in England and Mother didn't bring us to Toronto until 1928, and he died in 1939. As I say, Louella saw more of him than I did."

The absinthe seemed to precipitate a wheezing attack. "I always suspected he was something like Oscar Wilde. A thin Oscar Wilde," she added. "You know. Liking to hold court, tell stories, have elegant people around him."

"Do you recall him ever talking about Phillip Pariston, ever mentioning him?"

She shook her head and I could see she was beginning to tire, her eyes fluttering closed, her chin settling into the nest of bright silks. I asked her if I might spend some time in the study.

"The boxes of his photographs are under my work table." She told me that she had donated the original plates to the City of Toronto Archives. "I just don't have the space to keep it all."

There seemed to be no order to the photographs in the boxes. There would be one or two from his once-acclaimed lakeside series. Men in bathing suits creating a shaky human pyramid at Scarborough Beach Park. Children clustered around a street musician at Sunnyside. Next to these would be portraits of affluent Torontonians from the turn of the century, women choked with jewels and bows, Gibson girl hairdos sweeping up into massive feathered hats, vested men in starched collars. There were a few from his visits to the French Quarter in New Orleans and Central Park in New York. Other photos were from the '20s and '30s, starch and lace giving way to a kind of looseness in clothing and boldness of design that I could imagine Radcliffe Malthus enjoying a good deal. There were pictures of Toronto streets and buildings, and photographic records of political rallies, exhibitions and festivals. It was a shuffled deck that I sorted through carefully but I could determine no photos of Phillip Pariston or the art studies he referred to in that April entry in his journal before pages were razored out.

On the walls of the study, copies of some of the same prints I had seen in the boxes had been framed and hung alongside pieces of Edith Bircombe's works on silk, and mementos that suggested some time spent where? The Far East? Indonesia? Puppets, fans, elaborately cut paperwork. The room was beginning to darken in the lateness of the afternoon. As I sought a lamp to turn on, wondering how the drawing lights on her table worked, I sensed her presence at the door, confirmed by the slight mechanical noise of the oxygen apparatus and the pulse of her wheezing.

"He was a wonderful photographer." She struggled to find breath for her words. "I love that one with three girls and their bicycles. All gangly legs and spokes and circles. The design." She waved the hand not supporting the canister in airy circles.

"Is this a complete set of his work?"

"Heavens, no," she whispered. "Some things I don't think he kept copies of. Just the showier pieces. And then that Carroll got to his things before anyone else. I think some of his prints were spirited away."

"Carroll?"

"Uncle Radcliffe's secretary when he died."

"Does she still live in Toronto?"

"He."

"He?"

"Carroll Carmody. I think it was a stage name. He was an actor for a while in the '30s before Uncle Rad took him under his wing. He was very kind to young men." It was a knowing statement and Edith Bircombe glanced at me quickly to see what effect it had created. I raised my eyebrows a touch, enough to indicate interest, not enough to express shock.

"He's still around as far as I know," she said. "I think he lives comfortably off what Rad left him."

CHAPTER 15

AT A CAFÉ ON CHURCH STREET, I CHECKED A phone booth and found a Carmody listing for an address just north of Bloor and Church.

"You're not the first to be doing research on Malthus," a mellifluous voice informed me. "Are you coming from the art angle or the history angle? Someone a couple of years ago was thinking of doing some kind of a photographic history of Toronto. But it's not that easy to get rights to some of his stuff ..."

He was a talker, I realized with some relief, gliding from topic to topic—the copyright on Malthus's photos, the many disservices "Beady Edie" had done her uncle, tourism in Toronto, the weather. He agreed to meet me at Buddy's, a bar on Church Street, later in the evening.

Even after poking my way through dinner and reading a couple of chapters of an E.M. Forster novel I'd brought with me, I was still early getting to Buddy's. The bar was busy, a mix of men, a hubbub of chatter, canned music, laughter, the air infused with smoke and overhead lighting glinting off glasses. I spotted a couple of seats not far from the entrance, claimed one, and slipping off my blazer, draped it over the other.

By the time Carroll Carmody arrived, I was nursing a second gin and tonic. Even though we hadn't discussed how we would find one another, he zeroed in on me within seconds. But then I was one of the few drinking by myself.

"Curtis from Alberta?" He had a slight lisp.

Rising, I shook his hand—pudgy fingers, a bit moist, three rings, one with a large green gem.

"Carroll ..." I retrieved my blazer and gestured to the seat.

"So ..." He let the word roll so that it became almost an exhalation, a sigh. "A traveller in the world of art. I, too, have been a connoisseur. Drama for me, but that's art too, isn't it?"

He was a man who, I suspected, had once been strikingly handsome but whose early good looks had slipped away with the weight of years. One of the buttons on his patterned silk shirt had given up the struggle to remain secured. His over-coiffed hair was bottle blond and his deep-set green eyes with their long, dark lashes had a studied, exotic look.

He caught the attention of a waiter and ordered a double scotch.

"An artist with an interest in Radcliffe Malthus. I knew him well. His secretary, you know, for five years before he died."

"There's a connection," I said, "to an aunt of mine."

"Ah." Again, a reflective sigh. "He was a man of

connections." The scotch arrived and we raised our glasses in a salute.

"Of course, he was a crusty old bastard in his last years. But my gracious, the stories he could tell you about Toronto in the early days. And he lived it all, I tell you, Curtis." Carmody reached over and clutched my arm. "I mean he wasn't just there—he lived it! In with the Arts and Letters Club. The Masseys. The Harrises. The Group of Seven. Tom Thomson. He knew them all. Mind you, although he admired their work, he wasn't into what he called the 'school of canoe paddle painting.' Boating through the wilderness to find the perfect dead stump or wind-blasted tree. He used to say there's more poetry in a man with good limbs than any jack pine he ever stumbled across. This scotch is quite wonderful."

He drained the swallow remaining and I signalled the waiter for a refill.

"Brandy for me." It seemed right. Aunt Harriet's drink, of course.

We settled into the evening, becoming one with the hum of the bar, its dark rubble-stone walls, its smoke and music. At times, men stopped by to chat briefly with Carmody, obviously a regular. I felt I was being sized up as his companion.

"Did he ever mention a young artist—Phillip Pariston—actually a shirt-tail relative who stayed with him for a while during World War I?" I asked during a rare pause in Carmody's loquacious reminiscences. "I think he was a part of a group that met for drawing and photography. The Wednesday Club?"

"I don't recall the name. But he did talk about the men who met on Wednesdays back in the day. Men and boys. He'd studied under Eakins in Philadelphia, you know, and from him he'd learned to photograph the nude. Eakins's students posed for the master and they'd shuck their briefs in a trice if he asked them to. But say, come and see some of the photos I salvaged from the clutches of Beady Edie. Maybe tonight?" He raised an eyebrow.

I glanced at my watch. It was just after midnight. I didn't really want to spend the early hours of the morning with him. He was obviously working up to something more than a nightcap and a viewing of Malthus's photographs.

"I think I'd better call it a day ... er ... a night. Maybe a rain check? Tomorrow? I'm hoping to visit Malthus House tomorrow and I think the shack where Tom Thomson painted is available somewhere for viewing ..."

"We'd need to take a trip to Kleinberg to see a replica of his shack." Carmody leaned in, a pudgy hand again on my arm. "But I'll be your guide at Malthus House. And I'll ask my friend Moira to join us. She's a Thomson fanatic too so you should hit it off. I literally tripped over her in the McMichael Gallery a few months ago. I'm afraid we toppled a rack of calendars in the gift shop but we became—you know—instant friends. You'll like her."

We agreed to meet at Malthus House at noon the next day, both of us a little wobbly as we headed different directions on Church Street.

A THUNDERSTORM RUMBLED THROUGH TORONTO JUST after I got back to my hotel, and by morning, a heavy, moist heat enveloped the city. Malthus House was not a long walk but I was already mopping perspiration from my face by the time I got there, wishing I had left my briefcase in which I'd tucked the copy of the Thomson to show Carmody's friend.

From the gate, I could see the building was one of understated elegance, with a frontal arcade that made it look like something that might have rested more comfortably in the bright sun of the French Riviera than the shaded copses of Rosedale.

I found Carmody and Moira Greckel waiting inside the arcade where it was a touch cooler. She was a head taller than Carmody and, also in contrast, a thin and angular study in white, black and red. Pale skin, long black hair, black dress and pumps, lipstick as red as ketchup.

After introductions, Carmody immediately ushered us into the building and through what must have been a conservatory onto an adjoining patio serving as a restaurant.

"Memories," Carmody said, after we'd ordered our tea. "I've spent a few hours on these flagstones."

His companion raised her painted eyebrows.

"I said flagstones, darling, not fagstones." He gave her a playful slap.

"Moira's quite enjoying being a fag hag these days," he explained to me. "Expanding worlds. She's filling me in on postmodernism and I'm filling her in on post-Stonewall points of interest."

Moira Greckel winked at me. "I'm dying to see the Thomson," she said. Her voice had the controlled throatiness of someone equally comfortable giving a gallery lecture or ordering a cranberry scone.

"Ah, yes," she said, holding the colour photograph I retrieved from my briefcase. "Definitely from 1916, I'd think. Do you realize the treasure you have here?"

"Moira's doing her doctoral thesis on Thomson." Carmody settled back, with a cigarette, into the patio chair. "Something on the iconography of the tree. Right, darling?"

"It's fascinating." She flicked a straying strand of her Morticia hairdo back over her shoulder. "All that business with trees. It's all wrapped up with colonialism. You know what I mean—taking over the trees." She held the Thomson photo at arm's length and dug a pair of glasses out of a large black straw handbag.

"Of course, Thomson often focused on the isolated tree. Totem, crucifixion pole, or—as I've said—the terrible signature of the colonist."

"Moira can get more mileage out of a stump than ..." Carmody's sentence trailed into his teacup.

"I'm reminded," Moira said, as if the thought might just have come to her, "of some of the landscapes you see in battlefield paintings from World War I. Something from Flanders, contorted trunks ..."

"Thomson's tree does have foliage," I said, tracing the masses of verdure in the print that Moira had returned to the table.

"But dark and flat as bloodstains," she countered. "The only life is in the trunk—and there's comment in the branches."

"Supplication and distress?"

Carmody seemed relieved with the arrival of our food. "Would you believe I actually used to have toast and tea out here in the summer, catching up with Radcliffe's correspondence? Poor man. He was nearly blind the last year or two so he had no idea what I was writing. Would sign his name to anything."

Moira broke her scone into crumb-sized bites. "He was murdered of course."

"Murdered?"

"Thomson."

"Oh yes," I said, slathering jam onto a crumpet. "One of the Canoe Lake summer residents. A belligerent German ..." I scoured my memory for the name I had read in a biography of Thomson.

"Oh no, my dear," Moira scolded. "Discounted. Totally discounted. Everyone's certain it was the owner of the lodge, Probably manslaughter though, not actual murder."

Carmody's attention was wandering, I could see, and he looked impatiently at Moira's remaining pile of scone crumbs. "Nibble up, darling," he said. "I want to show Curtis the rest of this old shack."

WE ENDED UP BACK AT CARMODY'S APARTMENT AFTER A supper downtown during which we managed to kill two bottles of overpriced wine. Visa bills, I had decided fatalistically, were a fact of midsummer, and not something to be fretted over in the heat of holidays.

Carmody's apartment was cool, but at the price of an intrusive air conditioner. Moira sat in a spot that allowed the air stream to play on her long hair.

"Oh my god, that feels delish," she murmured, letting the straps from her dark cotton dress slip off her shoulders.

I sank into a chair opposite. Carmody was busy in his galley kitchen, visible through a counter-height opening. The living room, which had the unsettling appearance of a second-hand shop, began to acquire features. I realized that behind the bric-a-brac, plastic statuary, fringed lamps and wanton plants of a number of ivy families, there was actually a series of male nudes among photographs on the wall behind the sofa where Moira sat. One, I guessed, was a study of a much younger Carmody himself, fully displayed.

He peeked in from the kitchen. "Ah—you've found it," he giggled. "I was twenty-two."

"You haven't changed a bit." Moira's red lips tipped into a smile as she lit a cigarette.

"Liar. Margaritas coming up." He sang out. The sounds of a blender rode in on the base noise of the air conditioner.

As I allowed my gaze to wander from the nude photo of Carmody to others on the wall, all different models, all young men, one, I knew with sudden certainty, was Phillip Pariston himself, leaning against a pillar in the midst of hothouse greenery, a lazy smile on his lips.

"Who's that?" My voice came out as a squeak.

"Where?" Carmody emerged with a pitcher and glasses on a tray, pushing aside a pile of *After Dark* magazines to set it on the coffee table. I walked over, and through a smudge of Moira's cigarette smoke, pointed at the photo, partially hidden by the leaves of a trailing philodendron.

"Oh—just one of the models the Wednesday Club must have hired. Posing for sketches and paintings and photo studies. From back in the '20s I think."

"He's the one," I said, "the one I asked you about. Phillip Pariston."

"Really." Carmody took a closer look. "Interesting. So not a paid model—a volunteer?"

As Carmody and Moira sipped their margaritas, I filled them in on Pariston's journal and its missing pages.

A smile grew on Carmody's face as he licked salt from the rim of his glass.

"It's not the only one. There's more of your man," he said. "I rescued all the naked boys before Edie could get hold of them. I have a stash, probably worth some money these days if I ever choose to sell them."

"Shame about the part missing," Moira lit another cigarette. She could see I'd lost her train of thought. In fact I could think of nothing but Carmody's cache of photos.

"The part about Thomson," she added. "Missing from the journal. Might have shed more light on his last days."

Carmody replenished our margaritas and then hunkered down to pull a large box out from between a credenza and a stand supporting a Boston fern.

"You look through." He caught his breath as he got back up from the floor with some trouble and sank onto the sofa beside Moira.

Although the photos in the box were a jumble, the ones of Phillip were not hard to find. I pulled them out and arranged them on the rug. A variety of poses. All nude. In some he smiled, in others he was not really solemn but pensive. In a couple he seemed to be making love to the camera.

Moira nudged the one closest to her foot and picked it up. Carmody pinched a corner of it and wiggled it into a better light.

"Look at that cock. Can you imagine getting your mouth around that?"

Moira gave him a playful slap, careful not to spill her drink. "Less romanticized than Von Gloeden's photographs," she observed. "Although that man's handsomeness gives them a kind of veneer of romanticism, and the Malthus House conservatory has all the trappings of neoclassicism that Von Gloeden loved. You know the photos I mean. Surly Sicilian farm boys trying to look like house slaves. Everything hanging out." She gestured for me to hand her some more of the photos. "God, he was handsome."

"Now, my dear," Carmody said, sinking into the sofa, "give me your honest opinion. Is this not a man who has been experiencing the pleasures of the flesh with others of his own gender?"

"It's an assumption ..." I reclaimed my chair.

"Of course it's an assumption, or more accurately ..."

Carmody held a hand to his head as if multi-syllabic words were somehow taxing it. "It's a deduction. We're deducing from the evidence, from what we see in the photographs. Look at the eyes, the mouth, the unfettered sexuality." He stopped on the word, savouring it although he had experienced some difficulty in actually saying it. "Sensuality," he added.

"I'm afraid I agree with Carmie." Moira reached over and patted my arm. "Photographs do give us a picture even if they don't always give us the whole picture."

"You've nailed it. I agree with you both. There is sensuality—I think he had an artist's appreciation of its power and the time he spent at Malthus House brought it all to the front."

"I'll say." Carmody snorted. "Full frontal."

"But his love for Harriet didn't diminish ..." I wasn't sure why I was making a case for Phillip's virtue to people who had never read a word of his diary or heard Aunt Harriet's declarations.

"Confusion," Carmody said. "We have all known confusion. I, myself, for a brief period—when I was twenty—fell victim to the charms of a young woman who played ingenue parts for a couple of years before relinquishing the smell of the greasepaint and the roar of the crowd for the aroma of polished Rosedale mahogany and the gossip of bridge clubs. She married a lawyer and settled into a life of predictabilities, but she had been a wonderful Kaye in *Stage Door,* and, as I say, for a while I was quite smitten."

"Carmie." Moira was patting his hand now.

"And the point of all this, of course ..." Carmody refilled our glasses. "Is that, at the right time and place, it is quite possible to fall in love with anyone. Gender becomes a secondary issue."

"My point," I mumbled.

"But it had no future." Carmody leaned suddenly toward me sending a small wave of margarita overside onto the carpet. "It sorts itself out, with time—and generally not very much time."

"Cerebral love," Moira announced rather fuzzily, "cerebral love is powerful but temporal unless it is aligned to a physical disposition." The margaritas had not seriously impaired her ability to summon the language of the Ph.D student to her lips. "Cerebral—and idealized. Take Ruskin—"

"Ruskin!" Carmody giggled, and then whispered loudly to me. "You can count on Moira to slip a little Ruskin into any conversation. You did your M.A. thesis on Ruskin, didn't you dear?"

"I'm talking about the idealization thing," Moira pouted. "And Ruskin is a perfect example. He married, believing that women, like Greek statues and Victorian paintings, had no body hair. He was never able to reconcile ..."

"Hair." Carmody rolled his eyes. "Well—I guess we are talking about secondary sex characteristics. Or are we?"

"I'm not sure," I said. I traced my finger along the edge of one of the photographs. "And I'm not even sure it's cerebral." I shrugged and nodded to Moira. "I think it may be more subconscious. An accumulation of all the romantic songs and movies and magazine advertisements and wedding photos. Our desires, I think, are shaped subconsciously in ways that we discover sometimes collapse against the realities of our nature."

Moira had edged over to me and clasped my hand. She had long lacquered nails, I noticed, that ended with white crescents.

"Exactly," she said, in a little whisper that was more Marilyn Monroe than Germaine Greer. "Do you think Thomson's trees are phallic?"

"Oh, God!" Carmody exploded and lurched across the room toward the kitchen where we could hear him splashing more liquid into the blender.

"Lawren Harris's," I said, "might be considered phallic. Thomson's are more ..." I searched for the right correlation. "More androgynous, like hair. Tangled. Matted."

"Postcoital." Moira decided.

BEFORE THE EVENING WAS TOTALLY WASTED, MOIRA, who was meeting with one of her students the next morning, headed home, picking her way to the door carefully through the photos still on the rug.

On my way to Malthus House I had passed a liquor store and picked up a bottle of the scotch Carmody favoured. I fished it out of my briefcase now and gave it to him.

"A small gift. For allowing me to see these. To fill in ..." I searched for words. "... some blank spaces."

"Dear boy." He reached up a hand for me to help him up from the sofa, then worked his way carefully along

GLEN HUSER

pieces of furniture to the credenza where some liquor glasses nested alongside a cut-glass decanter. He broke the seal on the scotch and poured us each a good-sized portion.

"Choose two to keep."

190

CHAPTER 16

I T WAS AFTER MIDNIGHT WHEN I GAVE WALTER A call from my hotel room, just after ten, I knew, in Edmonton.

"Hey, Curt-man." Walter's voice, as it usually did, came in a decibel or two louder than most people's. "So, tell me, what's up?"

"Remember the conversations we've had about Phillip and those missing pages in the diary?" I said. "Well, as much as I hate to admit it, I think you might have been on the right track regarding Phillip and the Wednesday Club. There might have been reasons for Phillip to get rid of those pages himself."

"Tell! Tell!" It was the closest I had ever heard Walter come to squealing.

I reviewed my day and its escalation of revelations.

"Wow," was all Walter could muster at first.

"This Carmody guy—I think he was Radcliffe's lover

for a few years before he died. I guess he had quite an eye for physical beauty of the masculine form. Radcliffe Malthus."

"Did he make a pass at you?"

"Carmody?"

"Yes—Carmody."

"Yeah. I was getting up to leave. But we'd had some whiskey nightcaps after a few margaritas and he didn't mind when I pushed his hands away. He still let me keep the two photos of Phillip Pariston he'd given me earlier."

"Wow," Walter said again.

"Yeah, wow," I laughed. "I feel like I've been travelling back in time and the tour stopped at a point of interest, you know, only the point is Phillip, beautiful and vulnerable and so alive somehow, with only the air of the conservatory between his exposed skin and Radcliffe's camera lens. God, it's exciting. You would not believe how this man looked, Walter. Those photos on my bookshelf are nothing. Nothing. Walter, you need to see these."

"Can't wait."

"I wish you were here."

"Me too. But it was good I stayed. I don't think my sister would have survived with everybody coming at her with their ideas about the reunion. Ideas but not much assistance. Can't meet your plane, though, when you get back. That's the first day of the reunion and it goes on for three more." There was a pause. "You've got those photos out, don't you?"

"When did you become a psychic?"

He chuckled.

We said our goodbyes.

I did have the two photos out on the bedspread. In one, Phillip sat in a wicker chair in the midst of tropical plants of the conservatory, one leg draped over the chair's arm, a hand resting against the extended knee of the other. It was the only photo I'd seen of him with his mouth open, caught in laughter, and I wondered if he were self-conscious about a chip in one of his front teeth. The hair on his head was artfully tousled and I could imagine Radcliffe himself brushing his fingers through it. Or perhaps the boy. Was it Andrew? Andy?

In the other print, he leaned against a truncated pillar in the studio, a large, draped curtain pooling against the ankle of one foot. He had one arm hidden behind him while the other reached to touch the top of the pillar. The stretching brought bones to the surface, the tip of a pelvis bone, ribs. His eyes were cast down, perhaps studying the pattern of an oriental rug that ran a few inches from his naked feet.

Seeing the photos, it was easy to understand Aunt Harriet's lifelong passion for this man. I closed my eyes and saw them making love like ballet dancers, every move shimmering with desire and music, and then the melody changed, hovering uncertainly in the air, the young, blond Harriet faded, and the boy wrapped his arms around Phillip so there was an echoing in form of shoulder and hip bone and the long sweep along the side of the thigh to the opposing line of the torso, and the dance, sinuous, swaying, continued. Nijinsky the faun, mottled with desire. And, when it faded again, I was there. My own cheek was there, so close that it seemed possible to reach through time and trace the line of the jaw and brush my fingers against his nipples and feel the stirrings of his desire. But the sensations of my fingers was from my own flesh, and it was the fact of this—along with an incredible fatigue—that brought tears to my eyes as I slipped into sleep.

I WOKE WITH A MASSIVE HEADACHE THAT STAYED WITH me throughout the plane trip home despite Aspirins and soda water. No Walter waiting to pick me up, of course. But there was a large bouquet of roses from him on my coffee table and their aroma filled the apartment. I moved the bouquet out onto my small balcony, mixed myself a seltzer and sank into a patio chair where I fell asleep.

As I awoke, the smell of the roses hovered, a summery perfume that made me think of another summer day, I believe it must have been in the holiday following my first year of teaching, when Aunt Harriet suggested we visit the gardens of the Legislature grounds. In our slow progress along the walks, we stopped often to inhale the fragrances of floral beds in the height of their brief Edmonton season. Somehow, probably at my prodding, we got to talking about summer in Vancouver and she recalled it was July when Phillip went back to Vancouver and discovered Edwina had been hoarding Harriet's letters. I could feel her grip my arm more tightly, making me a kind of ballast against the memory. "Why she didn't just burn them, I don't know. Kind of a British thing, I guess, a certainty that you will be damned to hell forever if you tamper with the Royal Mail."

"You were still in Montreal?"

They'd been there for a few months, she told me. She was plagued with worry over why Phillip was ignoring her. Of course, she didn't know he had been in Toronto most of the time she had been sending her letters to Vancouver.

"I had a breakdown." The hold on my arm tightened again when she told me this. "In Montreal I went a little crazy. I began crying and couldn't stop. I quit eating. I think I wanted to die."

Per was beside himself. On his day off, he took her to the closest hospital, actually an army hospital, but a nurse took her to see a doctor who dealt with soldiers suffering from shell shock.

"Dr. Bilodeau." She remembered his name. He put her in a sanatorium for about a month to see if he could build her weight up as well as try to help her recover from her depression.

"They didn't call it depression then, of course. We've gotten better over the years labelling our insanities."

Harriet thought the doctor hid most of his costs from Per.

"He told me that the violinists of the world were entitled to special concessions."

Per, she remembered, came to visit her almost every day, and the days she didn't see him, she suspected he'd given in to his bottle of whiskey.

"I think he was trying to pull things together," she said, and laughed softly. "A fine twosome, eh—a madwoman and an alcoholic."

Later, when we'd left the legislative grounds and gone back to Aunt Harriet's house, seeking the coolness of the living room, she asked me to read something from the summer pages of Phillip's journal. I chose one of the first entries beyond the little ridge created by the removal of the pages.

July 27, 1917

I have heard from Hat today, a letter arriving that's led me to believe that there have been many over the past months, all withheld. Edwina was out for tea this afternoon when the mail came, and it was probably a good thing. It gave me a couple of hours to cool off. If she had come home immediately, I might have run the letter opener through her heart.

"Where are my letters from Hat?" I confronted her when she drifted in in the late afternoon.

"Whatever are you talking about?" she said, bold at first, but when I threatened to take the whole business to Dads, she said, "It was only for your own good, my dear. I thought time—"

She had them in a chocolate box in her room.

"You are a woman capable of great evil," I told her, and she said some very uncivil things to me in return. I told her that were it not for the peace of mind of my father, I would never speak to her again—and choose the first opportunity to remove myself from her sight as well. I had supper brought up to me and have stayed in my room all evening except to check on Old Grand. For hours I have been reading your letters, Hat, and weeping, I must confess. I ache to be with you and shall send a wire tomorrow to let you know what has happened. You only

have to desire it and you shall be returned to Vancouver and my
waiting arms. Leave your father and come home to me.

Old Grand is a bit better today, I think. The doctor says he
has had a series of strokes, and he has difficulty communicating,
but when I told him that I would be seeing you again soon, Hat,
I am certain he said, "Good." Kind of a cross between a word
and a clearing of the throat, but it sounded like "good" to me.

"DID YOU NOTICE, CURTIS, HOW THE DIARY ENTRY
becomes, as it goes along, a kind of letter to me?" Aunt
Harriet's voice was barely audible. I could see she was
bone-tired from our earlier outing.

"I think it was a letter to you," I said.

"I never got the wire," she whispered. "Papa went on
a binge and knocked over the landlord's china cabinet,
smashing just about everything in it. They ended up in a
big fight, actually coming to blows, and we got evicted.
He'd also gotten fired, so we were living in different
rooms while he was looking for another job."

In a couple of days they were on the train again, heading east. Per had heard that, with the war on, there was
lots of work for longshoremen in Halifax.

"My life seemed to be filled with losses, and a draining away of my energy," she said. "I'd regained a little of
my lost weight—I still weighed about twenty pounds less
than I did in February—and I hated the gaunt face that
looked back at me whenever I looked in a mirror."

I asked her if she wanted me to go on reading. She
gestured toward the cigarette box and nodded her head.

August 1, 1917

The train ride to Montreal goes on forever. It feels like a good part of my life over the past months has been spent on coaches clacking their way across the continent. I watch out the window a world of summer unfolding across the changing geography; I write in this journal; I sketch to make the hours go by. Some young infantrymen have been very willing models, providing I give them my renderings when they are complete. They have been company too in the dining car, anxious it seems to reach Halifax and convoy across the Atlantic and then on to the battlefields. I have not had the heart to tell them about Everett, shell-shocked and crippled in a Montreal hospital. I have with me a copy of the fattest Dickens novel I could find in Old Grand's library, and I immerse myself in the world of the Nicklebys when I cannot sleep.

August 2, 1917

I've been able to find a room close to the hospital and went up to see Everett as soon as I unpacked. There is little visible damage, but it seems that Vimy Ridge has somehow sucked the true Everett out of him and left someone else in his place, a kind of vacant visitor whose eyes wander restlessly, as if assessing the possibilities of escape. His damaged feet keep him bedridden, but the sister on duty managed to tell me (I think — her English was as bad as my French) that the doctor feels they will mend now that the operations are completed.

I am not certain if Everett recognized me. When I held his hand, I felt that his wandering eyes focused briefly and I thought he squeezed my fingers, but he says nothing.

When I got back to my room, I was seized with a fit of weeping. It is hard to make sense of this war, and to see those such as Everett made into husks of the men they truly are. When I think of how close I came to joining up myself, I feel I have been given a reprieve of sorts, and value each day for the fact that it is untainted by anything so dreadful as whatever cut into Everett's soul.

I thought of hiring a car to take me to the address on Hat's letter, but I shall rest for a while first. My nerves are in great agitation. Writing helps, and I have Old Grand's remedy of hot tea and brandy to settle me before I meet Hat.

I think of our last meeting and remember it being dismal and raining. But your eyes were shining—luminous, wet shining. All that makes the thought bearable is the remembrance of your eyes, my darling.

"My eyes," Aunt Harriet whispered.

CHAPTER 17

NOT LONG AFTER MY TORONTO VISIT, MY MOTHER came into the city for an operation about which she was very close-mouthed.

"They find things," she told me, "and think they should take them out. I wouldn't bother, but your father is quite insistent. What did people do before they had all this modern surgery?"

"They died," I said. Walter had driven us to the hospital's admitting bay. From where I sat, cramped in the back of his car, I could see him in the rear-view mirror—rolling his eyes.

"Thank you, Walter." My mother winced as she got out. Most movements made her wince these days. As we waited our turn at the reception counter, she said, "Such good manners. I'm surprised Walter's not married."

"That's true," I agreed. "It's hard for women to resist someone who knows when to say please and thank you."

"Scoff if you like. But if he lived in Yarrow, he'd have been married ten years ago and would have three children by now. It's this city. People don't get close enough to find out what a person's really like. Take you and Bradley. Look at how soon Bradley was married and here you are single still. It just supports what I say."

"Need I remind you that Bradley and Bonita are in the process of going through a divorce?"

My mother pursed her lips and fished a plastic card out of her handbag for the receptionist.

"Are you able to charge your illnesses now?" I whispered.

"Hush," she said.

While she was getting settled in her room, I went in quest of a flower shop. When I found one, it seemed to stock blooms suffering from their own forms of terminal illness, but I'd lost my energy to look further. I found a rose that had the appearance of being recalled to life, settled in a snowdrift of Styrofoam chips within a glass vase.

"Aren't you sweet," my mother said as I gave it to her. "A nice room, eh?"

It was hideous but I smiled stupidly and nodded my head.

I helped position her table so that she had the things she needed at hand—a Kleenex box, the *United Church Observer*, a small photograph album with an embossed plastic cover, a Lloyd C. Douglas novel that looked as if it had gone through someone's wash.

"*The Robe*?"

They have a little library down in the sunroom. I read it years ago ..." She lay back and closed her eyes. "Sometimes it's nice to read a book again."

I picked up the photo album.

"Just my latest roll of film. There's a couple of pictures of you and Walter in there from when you took Dad and me out on our anniversary. Have you put on weight, Curtis? I didn't notice until I got the pictures back."

"The horrible truth is out," I said. "Waistbands are being let out. Gym memberships are being renewed."

"Oh, you're not fat." My mother smiled wanly. "But Bradley needs to watch. He eats when he's upset and that whole breakup thing with Bonita has put thirty pounds on him."

She was tiring I could see. We are not a family given to embracing or holding hands, but I let my fingers rest on top of hers, and she sighed with what I thought was a small demonstration of satisfaction.

As she fell asleep, I found myself thinking of Phillip Pariston sitting by Everett's bed, his hand resting on his brother's hand. When I got home, I found the passage in the journal.

August 9, 1917

I am reading Nicholas Nickleby *to Everett. It is difficult to know whether or not he is able to make any sense of the words, but I think he finds the sound of them soothing, and once or twice as I read passages with Mrs. Nickleby dithering about (I have to confess to using something of a twittery voice), I thought I saw a smile catch on the edge of his lips. I read aloud, as well, the letters from Dads and the few words Old Grand manages to dictate. I even read a letter from Edwina, although it is difficult to have her words even briefly in my mouth. I feel as if I am eating poisonous food.*

WALTER, WITH A GROCERY BAG IN HAND, LET HIMSELF IN while I was reading, gesturing for me to stay where I was on the sofa.

"You look dead," he whispered, "and I have all the makings here for Irish coffee."

Walter was in the midst of taking an evening bartending course from NAIT and I surmised this must be the drink of the week.

"Read aloud," he called from the kitchen when the noise of the egg beater had whirred into silence.

"No," I said. "You're sick of me reading this stuff."

"True—but I know you like to, the way you used to when your old auntie was still alive." He emerged from the kitchen with mugs wearing extravagant caps of whipped cream. "Extra trips to the swimming pool this week," he said. "How's Mom?"

"She's into her Martindale martyr mode. Refuses to push the button to call the nurse for anything. Grits her teeth and reads some ragged novel about early Christians in the Roman arena, where people really knew how to suffer."

"She's a dear," Walter said, licking at his whipped-cream moustache. "Now read. Seriously. Read."

"Really? Being at the hospital with Mom made me think of Phillip visiting his brother when Harriet was in

Montreal—you know, when he was still trying to find her. I was just reading this part:

I continue to search for Hat but all the directions I've pursued have led to dead ends. Yesterday I was able to talk to Per's boss but he could tell me nothing that I did not already know— namely that they'd had a fight, not just verbal but physical, and Per had left the job without saying where he planned to go next.

A letter from Radcliffe, forwarded from Vancouver, invites me back to Malthus House, but Toronto, I feel, is a finished chapter.

"And it's even more finished," Walter observed, "if you take a razor blade and cut it out."

I laid the journal back into its nest of Pariston papers, my hand brushing Walter's as he dipped into them, retrieving the two photos Carmody had given me. We looked at them often.

"It must have been difficult back then." Walter held the photographs closer to the lamplight.

"What do you mean?"

"Well, you know, difficult to admit to being gay or bisexual. Difficult to find fulfillment." Walter had recently come out to his family and the topic was one that was often on his mind—and on the tip of his tongue.

"We don't know that he was gay or bisexual," I reminded him. "We only know that he posed in the buff for his photographer cousin."

"Yes." Walter smiled that little smile of his. "The evidence is circumstantial. But—ooh—what evidence." He held up the photograph of Phillip Pariston seated in a full and unabashed display of his nudity. "This is a pretty racy photo for 1917. Very homoerotic, I'd say."

"In the eye of the beholder."

"More than that, I think." Walter picked up the other nude photograph and studied it. "It's not just in the eyes of the beholder, it's—I don't really know how to say it—a kind of attitude, I guess. A consciousness of the impact he would be making. Remember, when you look at the journal, the Wednesday Club was all men."

"You're probably right. But it could have been simply curiosity. He was still pretty young."

"I think he knew how good-looking he was," Walter mused. "And sure, he was curious. No doubt about it. We've all been curious."

"Maybe everybody just took turns posing."

"Yeah—maybe."

"Seriously," I said. "If you look at the photography of Thomas Eakins, he was posing nude himself and had his male students posing nude as well. The Swimming Hole—he photographed a tableau with his students and then painted from the photo. It was a way of studying the human form and getting it right. They were all very excited over what the camera could capture."

"I looked at your book on the photographs of Eakins," Walter said, "and I think there were more currents in the old swimming hole than 'let's get the muscles down pat.'"

"But then you're not an artist." I slipped the photos back into an envelope. From time to time I thought of getting them framed and hanging them, but then I would think of scrambling to hide them if my mother paid me one of her unexpected visits. "You're not an artist," I repeated, surprised at the pique I felt.

"But I know what I like," Walter said, arching his eyebrows, looking knowingly, maddeningly at me.

CHAPTER 18

TWO YEARS BEFORE AUNT HARRIET DIED, MY father gave me a tape recorder for a Christmas gift.

"Good as new," he said as I unwrapped it. "It was in a box with a bunch of records and a record player at the Goslin auction."

"Mrs. Goslin liked to tape her students playing." My mother smoothed the paper from the present I'd given her, a perfume that she liked but rarely bought because of its expense. "I don't know who's going to give piano lessons now that she's gone."

That Christmas night, when I played the tape left in the recorder, it filled the small space of my old bedroom with a concert of piano pieces—uneven, in places faltering, but somehow touching in a way that only another teacher might appreciate. At times Mrs. Goslin's voice, soft, encouraging, patched the pieces together. It was hearing her voice, I think, that brought to mind the possibility of taping Aunt Harriet. Of preserving her own story.

Would she allow herself to be recorded?

"Lord, Curtis," she mused. "I can't imagine why you'd want my old voice ..."

But I could see that she could imagine, that she was intrigued.

"It'll probably sound awful," she laughed. "Like one of *Macbeth*'s witches."

"Well, let's test it." I positioned the microphone on the bureau close to her armchair.

It wasn't quite the voice that had charmed my ears in that childhood visit fifteen years earlier. But it was close. A little throatier now, an edge to it in places like brittle paper, but paper quickly smoothed. The laugh still tinkly, infectious.

In that trial run she recalled a time when she and Phillip had visited Vancouver's Chinatown. Phillip was in quest of ink and brushes, but a merchant, a plump, smiling-Buddha of a man, kept steering him to a display of fans and hairpins and brooches. In broken English and extravagant gestures he indicated Phillip should not leave without buying something for his lady.

"He had us both laughing. Oohed and aahed and clapped his hands when I tried a fan and then opened a parasol. We left the shop with our arms full, the shopkeeper following us to the door, shouting jolly things in Chinese. Could have been 'western fools!' for all we knew."

I stopped the tape and played it back.

Aunt Harriet was not displeased.

"I often wonder what happened to that parasol. It had a beautiful design of flying cranes on it. Somehow it got missed when Per and I left Mrs. Mezzkis's. I suppose she kept it herself but I hate the thought of that lacquered handle in her pudgy hands."

We didn't have a chance to try the tape again until a month later. We'd come back from a chamber recital at Convocation Hall. The music had put her in a melancholy mood, a mood anchored with my reading aloud one of Phillip's journal entries from the weeks he was in Montreal with Everett.

"When we first moved to Halifax, I didn't write any letters." Aunt Harriet eased into the silence broken only by the slight machine noise of the recorder. "I was truly despondent. Depression, I guess you'd call it now. It had been bad in Montreal and, not surprisingly, it came back on me with this move. I had trouble convincing myself to get out of bed in the morning, and sometimes I didn't—I'd just stay in bed for two or three days at a time.

"I can hardly bear to think of how distressed Phillip was, and how he thought I'd abandoned him, when, of course, I was certain he'd abandoned me. That first month in Halifax we were living in a horrid little flat in the North End. There was no kitchen—we were expected to go downstairs and use a common kitchen on the main floor. It seemed to take all my effort to go up and down those stairs and, when I did get to the kitchen and eat a bit, I wasn't able to keep anything down. One day I simply collapsed on the landing and Per called a doctor.

"To give Per his due, I think he was truly worried about me. He'd managed to get a job working as a stevedore at the sugar refinery wharf and he wasn't drunk as often as he had been those last few weeks in Montreal. Dr. McCormack told Per he needed to get me out of that decrepit rooming house. A woman who did cleaning for Dr. McCormack, Mrs. McTavish, had a much better rooming house a couple of blocks off Gottingen and her tenants in a bed sitting room with a nice view of the harbour had just given it up. Per even hired a car to get me over there.

"'Don't you worry, little magpie,' he kept telling me. 'Here you will be in good hands.' Mrs. McTavish's hands did look like they could handle most anything. Per stayed on at the rooming house on Veith Street and I think he worked extra shifts to pay the two rents.

"I believe we'd been in Halifax for about six weeks when I finally set pen to paper. I remember it was a very short letter, more or less saying that I just needed to know that he was okay. Well, you know what that letter meant to Phillip when he finally got it."

September 15, 1917

A letter, forwarded in Dads' handwriting—block letters for legibility, but with his distinct A's—arrived from Hat in the post today. For a few minutes I could not bring myself to open it. I have lived so long in the dark, unable to stop imagining the worst, that I believe I thought whatever illumination the words of this letter should bring, they might somehow blind me. I put it in my pocket and walked to the park. With the sounds of children chanting a French skipping rhyme and the slow traffic of the afternoon, I opened the envelope. It contained only one page—but for me it was everything! She is with Per in Halifax. Apparently well, although the brevity of the letter, and one sentence—"Today I went for a walk, only two blocks but came home very tired"—indicates she has not regained her vitality. I composed a cable and sent it within the next hour. We shall be apart no longer, I am determined.

When I went to the hospital, Everett's doctor sought me out and told me he felt Everett's feet are healed well enough that we might consider taking him home. It is great news, of course, but puts me in a quandary. I want to take him immediately but I also want to go to Halifax as soon as possible. As I think about it this evening, I have worked it out in my mind that I will go and collect Hat, return to pick up Everett, and then head back to Vancouver.

Ideas race in my head and I know I shall be unable to sleep, so I shall go out and walk now until I'm tired.

"I WAS SLEEPING WHEN MRS. MCTAVISH BROUGHT THE cable to my room. She was a big Scottish lady, a widow who'd raised her family with very little by the way of any frills and she'd never in her life seen a cable of that length. Of course, I began crying when I read it, and she wanted to know who'd died. A lie sprang to my lips and I told her it was from my husband. She left, shaking her head. At first Per forbade me to have any contact with Phillip, but when I told him I would run away if he kept that resolution, he relented. I think he was very worried over the amount of weight I'd lost and how ill I was.

"Phillip arrived two days later and the changes the last few months had wrought on my appearance, I could see registered in his eyes. He held me so closely, so tenderly, and we lay down and held each other, and both of us were weeping. I can feel the closeness of him this very minute, feel his arms around me." Aunt Harriet began crying as she told me this, tears slipping along her creased cheeks. I paused the tape recorder and lit a cigarette for her. In a few minutes, she sighed and nodded at the machine and I released the button.

"I thought I'd never see him again. Oh, Curtis, you can't imagine how wonderful it was to be with him. It was as if I'd been reprieved from a death sentence.

"But I wasn't well enough to travel so Phillip said he would take Everett back to Vancouver and then return. My mission, during the interval, he said, was to eat and get some exercise and build myself up. Papa came over a couple of times and had coffee with us. I could see it was an effort for him not to be flaring up at Phillip. In the end he kept insisting Phillip should come back and settle in Halifax rather than me returning to Vancouver. I guess he didn't want to lose me either.

"Although the station was only a few blocks away, Phillip wouldn't let me go to see him off. We had our farewell at Mrs. McTavish's. You can't imagine how hard it was for me to say goodbye."

The rooms in Mrs. McTavish's house were comfortable, Aunt Harriet remembered. "It was more like a small parlour with its own fireplace and the bed in a small alcove. When Mr. McTavish had been alive, it had been a room he had set up for his sister, but before I'd got my stuff unpacked, Mrs. McTavish had told me the full story of how she had lost both of them the same year: her sister-in-law to appendicitis; her husband, a brakeman, to a railway accident. It was a room with a bay window that looked out onto the street and the harbour beyond. Even before he left to take Everett back to Vancouver, Phillip began putting some of his sketches up on the wall.

"He'd brought me bouquets of late summer flowers and had done a sketch in chalks of some delphiniums. I was weak, but I was deliriously happy, Curtis. True to my word, while he was gone I made myself eat, and gradually, on Mrs. McTavish's sturdy porridges and ever-present potatoes and fried chicken, I began to regain my strength. I even began to practice the violin again, generally in the afternoon when I was certain it would disturb none of the boarders. I extended my walks, making it as far, some days, as the waterfront where I was reminded by the blue skies and gulls of a happier time in Vancouver."

CHAPTER 19

I N 1979, WALTER TOOK AN EXCHANGE POSITION TO teach in Australia. He was gone for over a year, a year in which we splurged on a few brief phone calls and exchanged letters—mine lengthy epistles, his much shorter. Walter was not a letter writer but what he did write somehow embodied him. I could almost feel the sand in his shoes, the heat of that southern sun on his skin.

On his return, we had a couple of visits over dinner and wine to catch up on our months away from each other. Then he dropped by unexpectedly on a Saturday evening when I thought he was out of town.

"Change of plans."

I had been making an effort not to have the Pariston papers or Phillip's journal out so much when Walter came over. Caught off guard now, the journal and some of the more complete sketches were on the living-room floor along with sections of the weekend newspaper and the tape recorder playing, Harriet recollecting Phillip's trip with Everett back to Vancouver before returning to Halifax.

Walter found his way through the maze of stuff and sprawled out on the sofa. He listened for a couple of minutes to the tape before I clicked it off.

"I wonder if he stopped to see one of those cute models in Toronto on the way back?"

"I don't think so." I set the recorder on rewind. "If he did razor out the pages, it must have been because he was remorseful about the episode and decided it was an aspect of his life he wanted to suppress."

"I suppose so. Or he may have been worried that Harriet would get her hands on it and read it at some point. If the pages weren't there, she wouldn't be able to read them. But that doesn't mean he would necessarily have given over what he found he'd acquired a taste for."

"I think he was in love with Aunt Harriet throughout all these months."

"I won't argue that," he said. "You'd expect he'd be pretty truthful to himself in a diary. Mind you, he wouldn't have been the first person to try and convince himself that he didn't have 'perverse leanings' or whatever they called it sixty years ago."

"The love that dared not speak its name?" The fact that Phillip had loved Aunt Harriet with such undaunted commitment made me question Walter's thesis, but I did wonder about what happened in Toronto. I had been reading a biography of Oscar Wilde and it seemed that he had a genuine love for his wife, fathering two children. Had it been a love such as Phillip had for Harriet? Perhaps people such as Wilde and Phillip gave themselves to many passions. There was that whole Victorian thing—still very present in the early 1900s—the romantic falling in love with love, the idealization and worship of women, not to mention the pressures of society to conform. In the language Phillip Pariston used in his journal, I sensed the power of these forces.

I retrieved a half bottle of leftover wine and a couple of glasses and put on a new recording of the Mendelssohn Violin Concerto in E minor. "It would be interesting to know ..." I portioned out the Merlot. "To know how their story might have unfolded if they'd been given years together—instead of months. And whether or not anyone would ever have been interested in them, apart from those with the most obvious kinship. Children. Grandchildren."

"You don't think he would have made his mark in the Canadian art scene?"

"Had his paintings hanging in the National Gallery along with Tom Thomson's and Lawren Harris's? It's hard to say. Maybe he would have become one of the legion of Canadian artists who never make the first rank. A couple of showings in small galleries. Teaching art at colleges or community centres. Doing a few portrait commissions. Or maybe it would have gone the other way. Maybe he would have been able to bring attention to figure painting in the way that Picasso did? There doesn't seem to have been much happening in that genre in Canada. With Varley, a bit I suppose. But not really until someone like

Colville and that's in the 1940s and 1950s. Maybe Phillip would have made it happen sooner."

"Maybe he would have been Canada's first gay painter."

"The older you get, Walter," I said, "the more obsessed you are with this ..." I searched for a word and borrowed one that made no sense. "Homogeneity. It shouldn't matter that much. I mean Michelangelo was gay and Leonardo was gay, but they're not thought of as 'gay artists.'"

"Interesting," Walter drawled, shaping the word with an Australian edge, "to hear you give me the gears about obsessions. Someone who's been obsessed for most of his life with an old woman and an artist who died twenty-five years before he was born."

"What are you getting at?" There were times when Walter and I had scraped at each other, but he was generally easygoing and seemed to find, almost effortlessly, what he wanted in life. Maybe the Australian sun had hardened him into something leaner and tougher.

"What I'm getting at is—where is your life, Curtis? Have you ever stopped to wonder that? Christ, half the time you're a shadow—not a person. Making the moves of that dead artist. Talking like him. Drawing like him."

We were both quiet for several minutes. I got up and turned the Mendelssohn over.

"The only thing you don't appear to manage," he added as if there had been no break in our argument, "is making love like him."

"I didn't realize you were that interested," I said.

"No, you didn't." He eased himself off the sofa, onto

the rug. "You make me think of Eddie, that guy we met at the bar at my bon voyage party. You remember? His whole life was streetcars. Knew every tram that Edmonton Transit had ever employed. Carried around pictures of them. I think he could have an orgasm from just touching an antique ticket box."

"Streetcars! How did we get into streetcars?"

"The same way everyone does. You steps up and pays yer fare."

"Don't be facile."

"All right. I won't."

He eased himself off the sofa and took his wineglass into the kitchen.

"Here, I'll give you a hand," he said as he came back and began gathering the Pariston papers, placing them back in the wicker suitcase.

"Leave the journal out. There's a part that's been on my mind, and I think I'll read it over later."

Walter was getting his coat.

"You don't have to go, do you?"

"Yeah, I better." Walter enfolded me in a hug. "I think I'm still a bit jet-lagged. G'night."

THERE WAS ONE PASSAGE IN OCTOBER AND TWO IN November. I read them in sequence.

October 9, 1917

Today Hat insisted I leave her to rest for the afternoon and go out and explore the city for a bit. She knows I'm anxious to find some studio space and so, with that motive in mind, I set off. The North End where Mrs. McTavish's house is located reminds me of the area up from the docks in Vancouver or, maybe even more, New Westminster, with its steep cramped streets and hodge-podge of houses. But the city does have a different feel to it, quite a bit more bracing with the Atlantic before us, not soft and damp. Even the fog seemed different in some way as it rolled in last night. Perhaps it's only that the blackout makes it seem different, the absence of streetlamps or the soft rectangles of light from windows.

No fog this afternoon though and Barrington Street bustles with activity. Trams and automobiles and cumbersome drays. I had coffee in a café after I'd walked for about half an hour and a young soldier with his arm in a sling joined me, intrigued, I think, with the quick sketch I was making of the street scene from my seat by the window. He has been in the Pine Hill Hospital but didn't recall meeting Everett, even though they would have been there at the same time, before he was moved to Montreal.

I continued walking to the South End where the houses are more like what you'd find in our West End, and the streets are lined with trees—massive horse chestnuts, maples, elms and limes. If I can convince Dads to increase my allowance I wouldn't mind looking for accommodation here. My studio, though, I think I will need to scout for closer to the docks where there might be a chance of getting some unused warehouse space.

Hat is looking better with each passing day and yesterday was able to walk, despite the steep incline of the streets, up to the public gardens at the Citadel, although we took the streetcar back, and she is tired today.

Halifax seems closer, somehow, to the war, and of course, geographically it is. I am reminded of it at every turn. Young men, many younger than myself, await transport, and the harbour is often filled with ships organizing to convoy. I know Old Grand is dubious about the motives involved in this conflict, and we are all horrified by the carnage, but I find myself consumed with a kind of embarrassment and mindless guilt as I go about buying pencils and drawing paper and making decisions about which ink is the best purchase when boys are perishing by the thousands in Belgium. The thought is more and more in my mind that I will be able, within months, to qualify as a war artist. I know the work I did at Spangler's studio has helped me to improve my craftsmanship, and if I do some work at the Victoria School and get a recommendation from Lismer I think I have a good chance of receiving a commission.

It will be hard to leave Hat again, but easy roads are accessible to few these days. Whatever the precipitate, the war has become a great consuming force with sacrifice at its core. It grows and continues to grow. Many of the soldiers I've talked to tell me they are going because of a slain brother or cousin or comrade. Not for the flag-waving. Blood begetting blood. The most important thing may be to make a record of this horror as it is happening.

In the meantime I find it difficult to look the men in uniform in the eye—and that seems to be a good chunk of the Halifax population. The terrible trip home with Everett remains a vivid imprint, those countless hours in a sleeping car, trying to talk to him, to find some word ember to which a connection might flare. Reading to him and wondering if there is any penetration of meaning. The return trip, while I found myself close to being ill with the repeated monotony of days of train travel, was a relief. I think I shall not travel by train again, though, for a very long time if there is any way I can avoid it.

"There's a terrible irony in those words," Aunt Harriet whispered to me once I'd finished reading the passage to her. "He would, of course, return to Vancouver one last time by rail."

November 9, 1917

I slipped away for a couple of hours this afternoon as Hat wanted to spend some time practicing. I need to spend time with Mrs. McTavish's piano too but didn't feel in the mood today. Restless, I guess.

As I headed to the harbourfront to have another look at the space I think I will lease for a studio, I noticed, through a café window, Per seated by himself. I smiled and waved and he beckoned me inside. He'd been doing extra shifts over the last few days and was having a late breakfast before heading home to sleep. He insisted on buying me a coffee.

"One of the few places where you can get a cup of coffee that wouldn't be better for slopping pigs," he grumbled.

"Not bad," I had to agree. With shortages, most restaurants were skimping but not this little dive tucked between two warehouses.

"The owner's a Swede." Per glared at the proprietor. "But his coffee ..." He made an airy, dismissive motion with his hand.

When he asked how Harriet was doing, I said she was doing well, improving every day, but it was as if he hadn't heard me and he said, "I shouldn't have brought her all this way. It nearly killed her."

I didn't say anything.

"You would have been good to her?" He looked at me as if the notion were something for which he actually needed affirmation.

"Of course," I said.

"Of course," he repeated, but with a hesitation in his voice. "This is more like home here," he said. "More like Norway. But she didn't need that—I needed that. Maybe I needed her too. She's all I have left of her mother. Sometimes we just think of ourselves."

I realized that Per had already been into his whiskey bottle, but only enough to become reflective—not morose or belligerent. Apparently he has a day off and I was relieved that I caught him at the start of it rather than at its end.

November 20, 1917

I am pleased with the studio space I've been able to secure in a warehouse, particularly as it is so difficult to find any unoccupied spaces with the war activity here. It has large windows and should be ideal for light. It needs shelving and a desk and work table so I've arranged for those. But first I think I'll paint the walls white—the place needs freshening. Hat is determined to help me and I shall let her come for a bit of it. She is so much stronger and has gained back much of the weight she lost since February.

Today's post brings a letter from Radcliffe. He says Barry has joined up and should be passing through Halifax sometime soon

and may look me up. I hate to think of him headed for that car-
nage. Radcliffe reminds me to get in touch with Lismer if I wish to
become involved with the Victoria School. He apparently is seek-
ing both assistance and students—and who knows, I may be able
to offer myself in both respects. I shall wait until after Christmas,
though, when I am certain Hat is fully back on her feet.

We had supper alone this evening upstairs. I have several
new records for the Victrola, so we dined elegantly on Mrs.
McTavish's Welsh rarebit, with Rubenstein's "Melody in F" in
the background. Hat sleeps now, and I will soon, but the love-
liness of the evening with a fire lingering in the grate, makes
me savour every minute of consciousness. Warmth and love and
civility and music. Are we an island in a large sea of disquietude?

BARRY. SOMEONE FROM THE WEDNESDAY CLUB? A FIRST-
name Barry, or a last-name Barry? Andrew Barry? Would
a check with the war records reveal the name?

Aunt Harriet could recall no one from Toronto looking them up.

"We lived very much to ourselves," she told me.
"There would be letters from Vancouver of course. To
start with we had meals with Papa once in a while, but he
began drinking quite heavily again and we saw less and
less of him. I think he had a ladyfriend who liked to party
with him. He let something slip about a Mabel or a Myrtle
a couple of times.

"I could feel my strength returning, and I didn't think
it was possible to be so happy. Phillip was so attentive I
practically had to force him to get out and begin doing
some things on his own. I didn't want to stifle him, and

I knew how important his art was to him, so I suggested he go hunting for some space for a studio. I began working on a couple of pieces, nothing too challenging—some variations on 'Greensleeves,' 'The Londonderry Air.' We thought we might have a little soiree in Mrs. McTavish's parlour for Christmas. Phillip had the piano tuned.

"None of this was destined to happen, of course." Aunt Harriet's voice faded out for a minute, then resurfaced, only barely louder, as she recounted into the tape recorder what happened on December 6, 1917. The first time she told me about it—before I had the tape recorder—I recall her actually pausing in mid-sentence and gasping, as if the waves of terror continued to assault her. When she talked about the explosion, her voice lost the resiliency I had come to expect, and the firestorm of the past had an undiminished capability of sucking moisture from her vocal chords so that her words fell like bits of burning paper.

"If there is a gift attached to my blindness," she whispered to me in those dehydrated, falling words, "it is that the last thing I was ever to see was Phillip sitting in the window seat sketching me where I lay, propped against pillows, drinking coffee. The morning sun seemed to spin gold around him with a kind of eerie beauty. He was absorbed in his task, but every once in a while he would look at me with the eyes of a lover rather than the eyes of an artist and smile. The Rubenstein piece we had been listening to a few evenings back played on the Victrola. Oh God, Curtis ..." I placed a cigarette in her shaking hand. "What did we do to deserve that? For one second, for a mini-second, a blink of an eye, Phillip was illuminated by a great light that shone around his head and torso, the part of his body in relief against the window. It was like a halo, a light beyond anything earthly.

"The glass broke first, flying at me in a thousand pieces, assaulting my face, and for a fraction of a second there was just kind of a massive whump and the noise of glass breaking and shattering against itself. Tinkling, if you can believe it, and I think I heard Phillip yell 'Hat!' but maybe I only imagined it as the sound, a kind of high piercing shriek followed by a roar rolled in, a wave of sound like a locomotive bearing down on you, and I felt myself flying, actually borne in the air. It seemed like a long time, being carried on this wave of grinding sound, like being caught on the breath of some gigantic, enraged monster. But, of course, it was only for a few seconds. And then my body found the earth, and breath left it, and it was all blackness. Nothing."

CHAPTER 20

I **HAD ALWAYS KNOWN ABOUT THE HALIFAX EXPLOSION.**
It was part of my family's stories. The story about what
happened to Uncle Hartley's wife, why she was blind
and her face scarred, why she remained shut up at home
and didn't come with him to visit us.

"It's too awful to think about," my mother said when
I was so young I could barely sift through details that
drifted along currents of adult conversation. But in time I
fit the pieces together. The most terrible explosion North
America had ever experienced. Two thousand killed, close
to nine thousand injured. Flying glass turning people into
pincushions. More blinded than Canadian soldiers in all
of World War I. Aunt Harriet among those left sightless.

We knew the names of the doomed ships. *The Mont
Blanc*, a freighter set to join an Allied convoy, and the
Imo, a Norwegian tramp steamer with a cargo of Belgian
relief.

"Just a stupid harbour accident," was how my father described it. "Mixed signals, you know. Think of the shipping channel like a highway. With lanes—these two ships in the same lane, blowing their whistles at one another, neither one giving way until it was too late, both finally lunging aside but in the same direction. Well ... they hit and even that shouldn't have been too bad except the collision made sparks. *The Mont Blanc* was a bomb just waiting to go off—all it needed was something to light the fuse."

Hartley had been in Halifax briefly in February following the disaster, waiting to head overseas. Always curious, I had pored over the letters he had sent to the family when he was in the army, letters my mother tied with a bit of Christmas ribbon and kept with her collection of photos in the bottom drawer of our living-room bureau. A few of them included newspaper clippings, yellowed and fragile in my fingers, about the explosion. One noted that more people died than in the Chicago fire, the San Francisco earthquake, or the sinking of the Titanic.

"I was surprised," Uncle Hartley told us during a visit once he'd returned to Alberta, "how quickly the railways and docks were repaired. There was almost no let-up in convoys leaving. Hardly any break in the business of war." His laugh was bitter as he shook his head.

From Hartley and our father talking over their beers, and the frayed clippings he had sent home with letters, the disaster was often in my thoughts. I tried to imagine the explosion sucking a tidal wave forty feet high out of the harbour, carrying off three hundred loaded freight cars on rail lines closest to the docks. But growing up in the midst of central Alberta with its small lakes and sloughs—and never having been to either coast—it wasn't easy to fathom such a magnitude of water.

Two hundred stevedores drowned.

"What's a stevedore?" I remember asking Uncle Hartley.

"A longshoreman. Someone working on the waterfront loading or unloading those big ships. It was what Harriet's dad did, what he was doing when Halifax exploded." Uncle Hartley sipped at his beer for a minute. "Incredible to think of the force. That one ship, the *Imo*, was thrown to the shore near Tufts Cove where most of the crew died along with lots of Micmacs in Turtle Grove. That was their reservation. Some of the survivors worked for me later in the brewery. Josiah—he lost one of his eyes and had a crippled foot but you couldn't find a better worker. I remember him saying all his children—I think there were three of them—died."

Other details. The roof of the railway station became a mess of twisted iron and shattered glass. An orphanage, the King Edward Hotel, and the Home for the Deaf became instant piles of rubble. The Acadian Sugar Refinery where Harriet's dad worked crumpled and burned. A mushroom cloud spread its plume five miles in the air.

Bradley and I knew about these clouds. We had seen a movie at school about the bombing of Hiroshima and Nagasaki. The show's narrator declared the world had never see the like of such a cloud before. I was ready to argue the point with my grade five social studies teacher but Mrs. Brinkley shushed me and said, "We don't dispute information from documentary films."

"Is it true that a doctor was seen carrying a whole bucket full of eyeballs?" Bradley asked Uncle Hartley on another of his visits.

"That's what we heard. Glass travelled with tornado force. Your aunt was lucky they didn't actually have to remove hers."

Our family chatter, along with Uncle Hartley's comments, echoed for me when Aunt Harriet finally talked to me about it herself.

"I'm not sure how long I was blacked out," she said. "I remember regaining consciousness and there was a kind of eerie stillness in which there were—what?—little flickers of sound, people crying, calling for help, the sound of tortured wood giving way or brick collapsing. I think I heard a crazed horse galloping by, and a dog howled somewhere off in the distance. I imagine my face must have been a mass of pain but, oddly, I don't remember being aware of that right away, even though I couldn't see a thing. Maybe the shock kept the pain at bay for a little while. I knew my face was a ruin when I ran my hands over it, dislodging slivers of glass, some of them becoming embedded in my hands. I felt my fingers covered with something fluid, and when I put them to my mouth, there was the taste of blood and something else—I thought it might be coal oil or gasoline.

"I remember screaming 'Phillip' over and over again, crawling over rubble, trying to find him. I heard someone groaning and I crawled toward the sound. 'He's alive! Thank God he's alive!' But it wasn't Phillip's hand I grasped. It was an old woman's. 'Phillip' I called out again. 'No—Madge. Madge Pattison,' the old woman said. I could barely make out her words. She was another of the boarders at the house. As I held her hand, I could feel the life go out of it.

"I found another body. It was the body of a child and my fingers discovered its cold nakedness and I remember thinking there were no babies in Mrs. McTavish's rooming house. Where had this baby come from? And then, as I kept crawling like some kind of sightless animal back and forth, cutting myself on broken china, impeded by the wreckage of the house's walls and shattered furniture and strewn bricks, I found him. He was dead, but my fingers discovered nothing that was shattered, nothing cut and torn as my own face was. Somehow in death he'd managed to stay as beautiful as he'd been in life. His hair was mussed and sticky with oil, to be sure; some of his clothing was ripped; but his forehead was as smooth as when my fingers had traced it in the night, the skin across his cheekbones untouched, his eyes open, his lips … no blood, just the oil that had rained down on everything. I took what was left of the sleeve of my nightgown and wiped all that oil off his face.

"Mrs. McTavish said his neck had been broken. She'd been away from the house that morning, over at Dr. McCormack's cleaning up after a dinner party he'd given the previous night. His house was on the South Side and the buildings there weren't demolished like those in the North End closer to the docks. Shaken on their foundations and all the windows blown out, but still standing.

"Mrs. McTavish joined the people headed along the streets to the north, aware, as they went, that they were heading into increasing devastation. She'd caught a ride part of the way with rescuers who had a tin Lizzie, but when they stopped to begin loading the wounded straggling southward, she got off and pretty well ran the rest of the way to her street. She told me later she'd stopped here and there to help some of the injured, calling to men to come to the aid of a woman whose arm had been severed; covering a man with a child pinned under him, both dead in their front yard; taking a teenage girl who was in a state of shock to where a cluster of survivors had gathered.

"The horrors along her route prepared her a bit for what she might find on her own street. When she found me, I recognized her voice. 'Oh my God, my God, my God.' Her chant joined other sounds—people running, the shouts of those trying to help the wounded, as well as the moans and cries of the injured and dying themselves.

"'My house is burning,' I heard her scream. 'Oh, my God! My house!' And then I think she noticed me stirring where I lay against Phillip. I'd wrapped my arms around him and was hanging on to his poor body as if it were a life raft. I felt her hands on me, pulling me away from Phillip. 'No,' I remember I kept saying. 'No,' and Mrs. McTavish said, 'He's dead, the poor boy. Let him go. Let him go. It's you we need to tend to.' And then she noticed the other bodies. 'Oh, poor Miss Pattison. And a poor wee babe.'

"She pulled me away from the building—I could feel the heat of the fire—over to where there was some debris from a garden shed. Some men came by and Mrs. McTavish called out to them, 'Over here, come and help this injured girl. She's been blinded.'

"'So's half of Halifax,' they hollered. 'There's a hospital wagon coming along behind us. Sorry, we can't stop.'

"Mrs. McTavish had found a blanket in the rubble and wrapped it around me. I remember I'd begun to shiver fiercely, my teeth literally chattering. She wrapped me up in the blanket and then held me in her arms as close to the warmth of her body as she could.

"'They're trying to free a family trapped in a cellar with their broken house burning on top of them. Oh God, human eyes were never meant to see such sights.' And then she was deliberately quiet and I sensed she was chiding herself for what she'd said about human eyes, knowing mine would likely never see anything again.

"It seemed to take forever for help to come. 'There's some of his things,' Mrs. McTavish said as we waited. 'I'll make a package of them. Here's a tablecloth I'll not be serving supper on again so it might as well be put to good use.' She tightened the blanket around me. 'You can take it with you. Everything's scattered to high heaven but there's his book he like to write in and some of his sketches. They're just a bit damaged.' She kept coming back and holding me, but then she'd spy something else and collect it.

"One of the neighbor women came along. 'Oh, Peggy.' She began weeping when she saw us. 'All Richmond's gone. Blasted to hell.' She'd tried to find her sister and her four children but it was like they'd never existed. Their bodies were never found, Mrs. McTavish told me later. Likely they'd gone down to the pier to watch the fire. Those closest simply disintegrated or were washed out to sea with the enormous wave the explosion created.

"Finally one of the wagons made it to our end of the street, a dray that was collecting the injured and carting them to whichever hospital was the closest, and Mrs. McTavish helped me up onto it. There were so many wounded on it that she couldn't ride but she walked alongside and somehow they kept finding room for another one or two of the injured on their way south. Some of the victims were people she knew and once, when we stopped to pick up someone, she whispered to me, 'Harriet, it's enough to break the stoutest heart.'

"Mrs. McTavish told me that I didn't utter a word throughout this ordeal, not a word since I'd cried 'No' as she pulled me away from Phillip. I thought I'd asked her about Per, about the men who'd been working at the sugar refinery wharf, but it must only have been in my mind. I overheard someone talking about it though—the refinery and the iron foundry and some of the other businesses along the waterfront. 'Don't be expecting anyone alive from anywhere along there,' I heard the driver say to someone else.

"The Victoria Hospital was wall-to-wall wounded so they took our wagon to St. Mary's College. Someone cleaned my face and I felt a doctor's fingers exploring around my eyes. 'There's nothing can be done here,' he told Mrs. McTavish, 'but I don't think we'll need to excise them.' They gave me a shot of morphine and I was lost to what was happening for a few hours. I was one of the lucky ones. I heard they ran out of morphine and ether before the night was over.

"Of course I heard about it all afterwards. No one talked about anything else. The worst blizzard in twenty years descended on the wounded city, adding new layers of misery. People perished in the cold of the tent city the army erected on the commons. Many died slow, horrible deaths, trapped in the cellars of their homes as coal fires from kitchen ranges and heaters kept the rubble burning. In the middle of that dreadful blizzard with its drifts of snow and howling wind, the North End was dotted with blazes burning throughout the night. Can you imagine it? The horror?

"Mrs. McTavish spent many hours at my bedside those first days at St. Mary's, and she would tell me what she heard at the doctor's where she was staying and what she read in the papers. Every visit brought new information. The search for survivors in the rubble throughout Richmond. Finding *The Mont Blanc*'s anchor shaft miles away from where the ship blew up. One of its cannons found in Dartmouth. Windows shattered as far away as New Brunswick. All those orphans dying ... my dad and everyone at the sugar refinery ...

"Curtis, the stories chilled our blood. I think those of us in hospitals were in a kind of shock for weeks, quiet in our pain, as if crying would be some kind of affront to, you know, the hundreds of dead. One day

Mrs. McTavish read me a little piece in the newspaper about Phillip Pariston, a young artist visiting Halifax whose drawings had been scattered to the four winds. Killed in the blast, his remains had been dug up from the Fairview Cemetery and shipped to his family for reburial in Vancouver.

"Mrs. McTavish, incensed that there had been nothing included about his 'wife' went over to the newspaper office and talked to a reporter the next day. Following her visit, there was another small article about his blind wife being hospitalized in St. Mary's College and how she liked to take out the few sketches that had been retrieved and trace them with her fingertips as someone described them to her. A few more of his sketches were found by people collecting odd bits of debris that fell for miles around, and some of these were forwarded to me. Mrs. McTavish would sometimes go over the bits and pieces of paper. She didn't like talking about the figure studies Phillip had done. She'd just say 'this one's naked as a jaybird.' I told her that artists study the human form as doctors do, but I don't think I convinced her.

"Finally, after a couple of weeks, I was told I was well enough to 'go home' but, of course, I had no home to go to. Mrs. McTavish had decided to leave Halifax but she saw me settled with a couple she knew who were taking in boarders. I didn't stay there long. The depression that had been with me in Montreal and when I first came to Halifax returned, relentless and soul-destroying. A doctor got me into the YMCA where they were tending to cases of shock—those who had gone out of their mind.

"Then one day I just walked away from it and that's when Jean found me—out on the sidewalk—and took me in to stay at the house where she worked. She said they could use another hand. I remember I said, 'A blind one?' and she said, 'Never mind, we'll figure it out.'"

"Was the fact that you were pregnant with Phillip's baby—was that a source of comfort?" I asked her.

"Oh yes." Aunt Harriet put her hand over her mouth for a few seconds. "I'd forgotten. Sometimes it's like a jig-saw puzzle, trying to fit the pieces together. Jean helped deliver him. I called her my little mother for a long time."

"SHE DID," JEAN LAUGHED WHEN I ASKED HER ABOUT IT. "She called me her little mother. I guess I was fussing like a mother over her wee babe and, with her being so helpless, I fussed over her too. She liked to have me do her hair and makeup for the evenings when she'd play in whatever little orchestra Emma Carter managed to get together. Lovely hair she had, kind of a whitish-gold colour and we'd do it with combs and a beaded headband that covered some of the scars on her forehead. She'd want too much makeup, though, I thought at the time. 'You look like one of those painted china dolls,' I'd say. Too much powder and too much rouge. She'd just laugh and say she might as well look like Madame Butterfly—hadn't her life been filled with misery and music."

Jean had been in Halifax during the explosion but it was something she didn't like to talk about.

"I wasn't where it hit worst," she told me once when I asked. "I was working in a place up on North Street. Doing housework. I was washing sheets and did get scalded, but it wasn't nothing compared to what happened closer to the Richmond yards. I've never had any trouble figuring out what hell must be like after that day."

THE PICTURE OF THAT DAY GREW AND DEVELOPED IN MY mind like a photo negative gaining more and more definition as it remains immersed in solution. The head of the bed, I knew, sat in a small alcove with just enough room for a night table.

"It was kind of a haven," Aunt Harriet told me. "I could lie there, just sleeping or reading, and sometimes I would just rest and watch the Atlantic sky with its bits of movement—clouds, a gull—caught in the rectangle framework of the window. I felt very close to the sky."

The adjacent wall was filled with Phillip's sketches, ones he thought might particularly please her eye. Chalk sketches of bouquets he'd brought her, renderings of the waterfront and beach, studies of her head and hands. Pieces he thought might offend the quick eye of Mrs. McTavish, he kept piled on the counter of the little oaken secretary. These included the figure sketches he'd worked on in Toronto, and more recent sketches of Harriet herself, nude or partially clad.

"He insisted on sketching Mrs. McTavish herself one day. I think he caught her scowling at all the pin marks we were making in her floral wallpaper. Completely won her over. She had it framed and hung over the piano in the downstairs parlour."

In my mind's eye I could see the wall of sketches, a

gallery of artists' paper yielding, only where it had to, space to a bureau, a dresser with an oval mirror, a washstand in the corner. The journal in its leather case lay on the small drop-leaf table.

"I thought perhaps he'd had it out during the night and had been writing in it, but there's no entry so he must have been reading it, or perhaps looking at the few photographs in its end flaps."

Phillip had gone down to the kitchen and brought back a tray with a coffee pot and mugs. He set his cup on the window seat as he sketched her. He would have poured her coffee and made certain she was comfortable against the pillows. I can see him reaching out and moving a curl of her hair in just the way he wanted it to fall over her shoulder.

He would have stopped briefly to wind the gramophone and set the arm onto the Rubenstein record before picking up the sketch pad again, then settling with his back to the double windows of the small bay directly across from the bed.

I wondered if, as he picked up his sketchboard and pencil, he might have happened to glance out the window, might have seen the munitions freighter and the Norwegian steamer moving toward each other. Ships in the harbour. They would only have registered as shapes, colour, pattern—a fleeting registry. He had already done two or three sketches of the harbour from that second-storey window.

"I heard the bells of the fire engine, but they were some distance away and Phillip was so absorbed in his sketch ... and then—it happened. The impossible happened."

CHAPTER 21

"**I** SUPPOSE CARRYING PHILLIP'S CHILD WAS WHAT really got her through those horrible months when she had to confront not only his death but the loss of her sight, and I think for a while, even her mind. When Phip was born, she must have had the care of him as kind of a return to sanity, an anchor."

It wasn't unusual for me to bring a dinner conversation around to the Halifax catastrophe.

Across from me at the table, my mother looked as if she were weary beyond measure of the retold tale of Aunt Harriet. She was in for a post-operative checkup, and she'd nibbled dubiously at a stir-fry I'd prepared.

"She said Uncle Hartley was smitten by Phip at first, and then he got around to noticing her." My mother stirred at the mention of Hartley's name. "I guess she was still pretty striking-looking, even with the damage to her face. I mean, when you look at their wedding picture—she was very tall and graceful and had beautiful hair."

I could see she was thinking about Hartley.

"In the dark, I suppose it didn't matter so much what she looked like." My mother put down her fork, moved aside her wineglass and poured herself a cup of tea.

"You mean 'what he looked like.' Uncle Hart wasn't exactly a lady-killer when it came to looks, was he?"

"I know what I mean. You think the sun rose and set on her, don't you?" she blazed at me. "I think you wish she'd been your mother."

"That's ridiculous." I cleared both of our plates noisily into the sink.

"There are things you don't know."

"What? That she and Phillip never married? What does it matter? They had plans, but just being together was what was important to them at the time. Aunt Harriet needed to become stronger."

My mother sipped her tea silently, refusing to look at me, and then she said, "Have you ever wondered how Harriet and Hartley met?"

"No—I haven't wondered because she told me. They met over a picnic in a park. He began playing ball with Phip."

"Ha!" she snorted.

I sat calmly down across from her at the table. "I want you to please tell me what you're getting at," I said. "I'm not going to rise from this table until I know what's on your mind. There's no need for you to be jealous of Aunt Harriet. I never wished she were my mother. For heaven's sake ..."

"Well, you should know that Hartley never met her at a picnic. He met her at one of those places men go to

... when they want to meet a woman. She worked there. And, you're right, his heart was captured by her little boy. But the little boy wasn't as old as you think."

"What do you mean?"

"He was born in 1919. I'm surprised you and Phip never had a conversation about that."

"No—he couldn't have been."

My mother looked up from her teacup and sighed. "I don't think Phip ever knew who his father was—and maybe Harriet didn't either. It certainly wasn't Phillip Pariston."

"MY TIME OF THE DAY IS THE HOUR BETWEEN MIDNIGHT and one. You can think of it as really late or really early," I had told my grade eight language arts class earlier that day as I reviewed an exercise I'd posed for them on biographical writing. "What choices define you? Choose a colour, your favourite food and drink, the clothing you prefer to wear, the time of day you like best. If you were to take one piece of music to a desert isle—what would it be? For me: black (I didn't tell them that it had been Phillip Pariston's favourite colour as well—a detail that Aunt Harriet had given me; that Phillip's diary had corroborated), crab salad, California wine, a turtleneck sweater, Bruch's Adagio, the hour past midnight."

They looked at me balefully, sadly, as they might view someone slipping, without hope of rescue, to the edge of a sloping world. And now I sat poised at that world's edge, confronting a sea of shifting waters, the Pariston papers scattered before me, drifting, sinking. Would it be possible to retrieve any of them? I saw the elegant curling words of Phillip's journal pages and, on loose, crumpled sheets—chalked limb, the twisted trunk, traces of clothing, seared edges and torn holes.

All the negative spaces.

Perhaps not all?

How much of it had been a lie? Desire hardened into dream-facts. Missing months congealed into what she wanted to be true—a child of her heart's desire.

Had Hartley deliberately let the delusion drift? Out of kindness? Not wanting to stir currents that no longer mattered, careful not to trigger another bout of depression? Some kind of pact between Hartley and Phip? And what about Jean—refusing to revisit a past that didn't fit with her Edmonton churchgoing?

Well into that hour past midnight, none of the sweet comfort of that quiet, gentle midpoint of the night came to me. There was a bitter taste in my mouth. I found a tape of the Bruch adagio and tucked it into the player by my studio bed but it failed to ply its usual magic.

"It was a piece I never managed to master, but I loved to listen to it," Aunt Harriet had once told me. "Phillip and I heard Antonio Scech play it at one of Edwina's soirees. When Dad and I were in Montreal those terrible first days—it was impossible for me to keep any food down, it seemed, but I remember getting dressed one day when there was some March sun and walking to a little bakeshop that had a couple of tables. I ordered café au lait and one of their freshly-baked croissants, and by sipping the milky coffee and eating tiny bits of the bun, I was able to keep it down, and I remember feeling so thankful. It was warm enough that the shopkeeper had opened the window a bit and, from a rooming house across the street, from an upstairs window—also open—someone was practicing Bruch's adagio. I felt it was a sign."

It had nourished me too, in small ways. The perfect music for midnight but now it seeped around me like a fine, choking dust. I poured myself a glass of the white wine we'd had with supper. One of my mother's concessions to this modern age was to take a few sips of wine with a meal. Her preference for something sweet and German always left me with half a bottle, for which I had little taste, in the refrigerator.

I retrieved it now and drank it like medicine. Fortified, I rapped on the bedroom door. She was a restless sleeper —a Martindale trait she reminded me often—and it was almost as if she had been waiting for me to knock.

"Curtis?" Her voice was tiny in the dark room.

I let a shaft of hallway light slice across the rug to her bed.

"How could you ever ..." My voice was shaking, ready to crack, as it had been when I was a child on the verge of tears. I stopped and took a breath. "How could you know such a thing? You made it up didn't you?"

"Hartley told your father." I sensed a note of regret in her voice, as if circumstances beyond her control had contrived to wrest this information from a securely-locked vault of family secrets. "One time when they had a little too much to drink." She was sitting up in bed now, and I heard her sigh. "Your uncle never had much what-do-you-call-it. Never thought girls—women would take a second look at him."

"Self-esteem."

"He never had it. Your father thinks he took comfort from the fact Harriet could never see him. I was so ashamed to think of him going to one of those places. I think they must be just in big cities. We never had anything like that around Yarrow."

"She might have worked there, but as a housemaid and … and playing in a little band. She played the violin …"

My mother closed her eyes for a minute.

"It was a long time ago," she sighed, "and it is true that Hartley was captivated by her little boy. Who knows …"

"She—" I'm not certain what I was going to say but my voice shuddered and cracked on the first word, and I felt the warm, acidy Rhine wine surge back up my throat.

"I'm sorry," my mother said. She was not a woman given to apologies and I knew how difficult it was for her to say these words.

"'S okay," I managed to say and closed the door before I threw up.

LATER, I CLIMBED BACK INTO BED, SHIVERING, MY HEAD pounding. The trick to falling asleep, I knew, was to force myself to focus on something free from any anxieties. "'Imaging' or 'visualizing' I believe one of our school psychologists called it during a professional development session he'd given our staff on 'Defeating Stress—Channelling the Mind.'"

A street light shone through the window creating a panel of light defined by a cross on the wall opposite the sofa bed. In the bottom of the quadrant the small Thomson painting assumed the colours of the night, the trees in the foreground darker, the blazing fall colours of the background muted to softer shades of gold.

I visualized being there, by Thomson's shoulder as he applied paint with bold strokes of his brush, sometimes—with just a touch of impatience—grasping his palette knife and manipulating the paint with that. I felt I could reach out and touch his checkered shirt. Somewhere on the lake a loon called, its sound echoing through the Algonquin wilderness. With the last ripple of sound, I conjured up the other figure, the young man, the beautiful young man, sketching by Thomson's side.

Thomson stopped and looked at the piece Phillip worked on and the young man said, "I know. I need to give over chalks and crayons, be bolder." There was a gentle self-amusement in his voice, and the words fell softly into the afternoon. It would be afternoon light. Afternoon light seemed right, and as the hour wore on they would pack up paints and chalks and brushes, secure the materials and the sketches in the panel box in the canoe, and push out into the lake.

Why not?

The stillness, the slow progress of the canoe across the lake became cushions against which I lay my head, rubbing out the pain.

And then, I could see them at the wharf—Harriet and her baby in her arms, waiting.

Let us reclaim the ordinary scenes, I thought, in these long minutes before sleep. Allow the momentum of life, pull the bludgeoned artist free from the water, let him hum "Annie Laurie" in the early evening air, let the young man step clear of the collapsing walls, let him greet his wife at the dock, relieve her of the child, let her see her husband holding the boy, gently rocking him. To sleep. To sleep.

But sleep, while it circled and teased, backed away from me. Maybe it would not be possible to win back lives this night. The crossed panel of light remained relentlessly on the wall. For the last couple of years I'd kept a bottle of sherry in the top shelf of an old glass-doored bookcase Walter and I found at an estate sale. I got up and poured a glass, weighing this indulgence against a likely resurgence of the headache and the effect it might have on my still-queasy stomach. I took the Bruch out of the player, replacing it with a tape I'd left out on the end table—a collection of ragtime piano. I turned the volume down to something barely audible, ragtime that would not reach to the next room and its guest who had the Martindale problem of elusive sleep as I did myself. Was it ragtime they played in that House? A Russian girl on an accordion? Harriet on violin? The piano player who came early to visit with the blind woman, read aloud to her from a cherished diary? In that house where Jean boiled the stained sheets and painted eyebrows onto the scarred face of one of the many who had come through hell and were scraping out a corner for themselves while the fire and brimstone was being banked for the night.

A piano player with something of the grace of her dead artist? Maybe not as handsome but what does that matter when you have no vision? A piano player who could not keep his eyes off this wounded woman who could summon familiar melodies on the old fiddle the house had to offer, dance tunes that paced the shuffling feet of couples in the parlour? Maybe once, during a break, she said, "Play the 'Moonlight Sonata.' Play Beethoven for me," its recursive notes smoothing the way, later, to her room where she lay on a rumpled bed while a dampness from her sightless eyes seeped along powdered scar trails. Did he kiss her then and make love to her in a way she remembered, so that she arched and cried and pulled the seed deep within her? And, later, didn't wash it away.

Oh, Harriet.

Hat.

Hat.

For her another beginning? But one she could layer onto an ending, in time refiguring it as a reality?

Morning is a strange territory. Its earliest hours, for the insomniac, are filled with restless fantasies. In this night of revelation, of half-dreams, I found not only the young Phillip and Harriet but I sought out Phillip again, an older Phillip, his handsomeness edged with circumstance, a man who, perhaps like Nijinsky, danced away from prescribed circles. For Nijinsky it had ended in sorrow and madness. Where would the dance take Phillip? In the early morning, I followed him to Toronto coffee houses where young Greek men met him, sharing cigarettes and, later, sharing the lips and hands that held these cigarettes. Or was it just one man?

Phillip.

Now, with the lurid red announcement of 4:37 from my digital clock in my peripheral vision, I let Phillip and Harriet go back to their secrets, their graves. And, lying in bed, the crossed panel dimming with the light of pre-dawn, I thought of Walter. He filled, I realized, the space surrounding me. Was it too late to let him know I knew this now?

I could picture him laughing.

"You always knew it," I could hear him saying. "But you have a way of not looking at things head on."

I wouldn't argue.

What would I do?

Maybe I would reach over and pull him so close to me he wouldn't be able to talk, wouldn't even want to talk. I would inhale the smell of him and trace with my fingers the trinity of small moles that nestled at the back of his neck, feel the ridge of his shoulder bones through the fabric of his shirt, touch those full Slavic lips in ways that would surprise him—and me.

Maybe Walter had been wrong. Maybe I had learned from Phillip Pariston how to love.

I closed my eyes. I may even have slept for a couple of hours.

BEFORE MY ALARM WENT OFF, I GOT UP AND MADE coffee as quietly as I could but, within minutes, my mother joined me in the kitchen, clutching around her the mossy green housecoat dotted with leaf shapes that my father had given her for their fortieth anniversary.

"Couldn't sleep," she said, searching my face. "You look like death."

"I couldn't sleep either."

"I'm sorry …"

"No, it's okay." I poured our coffees.

"It's odd, you know." She took a knife and levelled a spoonful of sugar before easing it into her cup. "I feel like some kind of weight has been lifted just letting you know things weren't quite the romantic dream you made out. It's important to be truthful …"

I grasped her hand. "I know. It's okay. I'm discovering that all the time myself."

She looked at me oddly, the idea jelling in her mind, I could see, that I would forever be a mystery to her. It was a fact she relied on that I never agreed with her.

In the small, magnetized mirror attached to the fridge door across from me, I thought I did indeed look like death with a trace of a smile on his face.

"What are you grinning about?" My mother was always suspicious of anyone who smiled in the absence of any obvious cue.

"Oh—nothing." I drained my coffee cup. "And everything."

Even though we were not a family given to hugs, I wrapped her in my arms before I left for school. Awkwardly she returned the hug and then brushed back some hair that had fallen over my forehead.

"Now you're all set," I said. "The cab will be here at 8:30. It'll get you to the bus depot in lots of time."

She nodded and forced a smile herself.

"Say hi to Dad from me—and Bradley."

A LONG NIGHT'S JOURNEY INTO MORNING. WEDNESDAY
morning. Wednesdays Walter and I regularly got together
after work for drinks and dinner at that café—our café—
at the south end of the High Level Bridge. There was the
day to get through, but with my classes writing exams, it
would be an easy day. A smooth blank page, I thought as I
caught my bus. Settling into my seat, though, I closed my
eyes and along the bottom of that blank page, tore out a
jagged, irregular piece, creating a shape that shimmered
with possibility. In my mind, I traced the random pattern,
reading with my fingertips, as Harriet Ahlstrom once had
with her own torn papers, a world beyond the surfaces.

BURNING THE NIGHT

AUTHOR'S NOTE

Burning the Night was shaped by the convergence of some of my life experiences with abiding interests I have had in twentieth-century Canadian history and art. When I was a teen I did learn, in bits and pieces, about Tom Thomson and the development of the Group of Seven, but I somehow managed to go through grade school without ever encountering information about the Halifax Explosion. I must have been in college when I picked up a copy of Hugh MacLennan's *Barometer Rising*. I think the climactic scenes of the disaster shook my own rafters a bit. How did I know about the San Francisco earthquake, the great Chicago fire, the sinking of the Titanic—and not know this? Easy answer: I'd seen the American movies that played the Legion Hall on Saturday nights in the small Alberta town where I grew up, or, once my family moved to Edmonton, on the first television we owned. I'm a compulsive researcher, and once bitten, I read everything I could find on that World War I tragedy in Halifax, adding, over the years, to a clippings file and a dedicated bookshelf.

As I trained to become a teacher in the late 1950s–early 1960s, I majored in art and studied figure drawing under the guidance of Dr. Henry Glyde. Taking a break after teaching junior high in Edmonton for three years, I moved to Vancouver for a year of courses at the Vancouver School of Art. Then I was back in Edmonton, teaching again but taking art courses when I had a chance.

Increasingly I became interested in Tom Thomson who died in a canoe accident (some speculate he was murdered) just before his colleagues adopted the name "The Group of Seven." In time I was able to view Thomson's originals in art galleries across Canada. His distinctive paintings of the Ontario landscape continue to mesmerize me, and as I did with the Halifax material, I gradually gathered everything I could find about the artist's life, his craft—and his mysterious death.

When I lived in Vancouver, I spent a good deal of my free time walking and exploring its streets, particularly fascinated by the remaining mansions once owned by those who had grown rich on the bounties of BC's forests and minerals and the port industry. What were the stories these houses had to tell? A staunch fan of historical fiction, I began thinking of shaping a narrative in which several strands might meld, settling on 1917, the year of the explosion and the year Tom Thomson died, as a focal point. Phillip Pariston emerged from one of those Vancouver mansions; Harriet Ahlstrom from the city's waterfront. On microfiche I delved into copies of the *Vancouver Sun* (1916–1917) for weeks on end, finding details, living the days. Microfiche also allowed me to roam through Toronto and Halifax. Nijinsky danced in Vancouver; Toronto artists met at the Arts and Letters Club; a ravaged Halifax chronicled its wounds.

DISCUSSION QUESTIONS

1. In some ways this is a "doubly historical" novel with parts set in 1916–1917 and other parts ranging over the 1950s to the 1970s. In contrast to our current time, what details are distinctive to these periods? Are there some aspects that resonate with today's world?

2. Major Canadian cities serve as settings from sequence to sequence—Edmonton, Vancouver, Toronto, and Halifax in particular. Do you feel the author captured distinct features of each? Anything missing?

3. What parallels do you see in Phillip's and Curtis's lives? How does Curtis shape his life to fit the Phillip who emerges from journal entries and Aunt Harriet's remembrances?

4. Through much of the novel, Curtis reveals himself as extremely shy and unaccepting of his sexuality. Projecting from the 1960s/1970s to the 2020s, do you think a Curtis growing up today would have been more comfortable with himself? Would Walter have been any different in today's social environment?

5. "Negative space" is a term artists use in composition, one that Curtis employs with his junior high art club. How does the term expand as a metaphor for other things happening (or not happening) in the novel?

6. We discover that Harriet can be unreliable in recounting some of her experiences. How do other characters choose to cover for her, and how do these choices serve to foster Curtis's unblinking acceptance of her stories?

7. Although there are hints early on about what happened to Phillip and Harriet in December 1917, why do you think the author chose to use the closing chapters of the book to detail the Halifax Explosion?

8. When did you first learn about the Halifax Explosion? Do you think this is an incident not very well known outside of Canada (and possibly unknown by many Canadians)?

9. How does music resonate throughout the novel? Were you spurred to track down and listen to any of the classical pieces mentioned? Which do you think would best

serve as a musical accompaniment for the "Love Has Me Haunted" poem that prefaces the novel?

10. Canadian art is another crucial strand in the narrative. What was distinctive about the landscape art of Tom Thomson and the Group of Seven? Is there any resolution today about the mystery of Thomson's death?

12. If you were to cast a movie of *Burning the Night*, what actors would you pick to play Curtis, Walter, Aunt Harriet, Harriet as a young woman, Phillip Pariston, Per, Edwina, Radcliffe Malthus, Tom Thomson, Carroll Carmody, Moira Greckel, Curtis's mother?

ACKNOWLEDGMENTS

I AM HUGELY INDEBTED TO THE RUTHERFORD LIBRARY AT the University of Alberta in Edmonton, which allowed me access to its newspaper archives on microfiche. I am also indebted to the many who have written about the development of Canadian art in the early years of the twentieth century, the life and work of Tom Thomson, the home front and the battlefields of World War I, histories of Vancouver, Toronto and Halifax, and the historic explosion there. Some of these key materials are listed below.

Edmonton colleagues read earlier drafts of *Burning the Night* and provided valuable feedback. Thanks to Caterina Edwards Loverso, Robin Hedley-Smith, Sandra Mallett, Helen Rosta, Ilona Ryder, Greg Randall, Kay Stewart, Dianne Linden, Jocelyn Brown, Norm Sacuta and Doug Schmidt. I'm grateful to NeWest Press editor Sheila Pratt for suggesting ways to tighten the narrative and strengthen character relationships. Thanks as well to my sister Karen McFarlane for her close reading and editorial notes.

When my partner, Ellis Canning, and I toured the Atlantic provinces in the fall of 2015. We were hosted in Halifax by Ellis's good friend, Wayne Rogers, who lives directly across from where the explosion occurred. Wayne drove us through the parts of Halifax that had been most impacted and we spent some time in the military park where a sculpture commemorates the disaster, watching the sunset over the harbour. I could breathe the air and walk where I had led Phillip and Harriet. Thanks, Wayne!

I am indebted to the Canada Council for the Arts for the grant I received as I embarked on this project.

Here are some of the books that served me well:

Bindon, Kathryn M. *More Than Patriotism: Canada at War 1914-1918,* Nelson, 1979.

Davies, Blodwin. *Tom Thomson.* Mitchell Press, Vancouver, 1967.

Kitz, Janet F. *Shattered City: the Halifax Explosion and the Road to Recovery.* Halifax: Nimbus, 2008.

Little, William T. *The Tom Thomson Mystery.* McGraw-Hill Ryerson, 1970.

Looker, Janet. *Disaster Canada.* Lynx Images, 2000.

Man Along the Shore! The Story of the Vancouver Waterfront as Told by Longshoremen Themselves, 1860-1975. ILWU Local 500 Pensioners, Vancouver, 1975.

Murray, Joan. *The Best of Tom Thomson.* Hurtig Publishers Edmonton, 1986.

Newlands, Anne. *The Group of Seven and Tom Thomson.* Firefly, 1995.

Rasky, Frank. *Great Canadian Disasters.* Toronto: Longmans, Green & Co., 1961

Smedman, Lisa. *Immigrants: Stories of Vancouver's People.* The Vancouver Courier, 2009.

Yesterday's Toronto: 1870-1910. Prospero Books, 1997.

From his earliest years, **GLEN HUSER** has loved to write and read and draw and paint. That's when he wasn't losing himself in the dark cocoon of a movie theatre or picking out old-time radio standards and Broadway musical hits on the piano. As a teacher and school librarian for a lengthy career in Edmonton, he worked his passions for art and literature into school projects such as *Magpie*, an in-house quarterly featuring writing and art from students. In his off hours, he wrote movie reviews for a local weekly, children's book reviews for the *Edmonton Journal*, and got his small ink landscapes into galleries. As he worked on a degree in Education and then a Masters in English at the U of A, he had the good fortune to work under the tutelage of Rudy Wiebe, Margaret Atwood, and W.O. Mitchell. For several years he was a sessional lecturer in children's literature, information studies and creative writing at the U of A in Edmonton and UBC in Vancouver. His first novel *Grace Lake* was shortlisted for the 1992 W.H. Smith-Books in Canada First Novel Award. He has written several books for young adult readers including the Governor General's Award-winner *Stitches* and the GG-finalist *Skinnybones and the Wrinkle Queen*. Short stories have appeared in a number of literary magazines, most recently *Plenitude* and Waterloo University's *The New Quarterly*. Glen's current home is Vancouver where he continues to write as well as pursue interests in art and film studies.